"Expecting trouble?"

Levi answered with a shrug.

Mara began to thumb through the files before piling them into one of the empty boxes. She thought back to the message she'd gotten on her cell phone. *Marbles.* "Hmmm."

Levi joined her. "Find something?"

"Not the appointment book, but a bid on a project to pour a small concrete patio." Her gaze met Levi's. "At Teegan's house."

"Date?"

"That part's torn off. This is just an estimate for the bid. Doesn't really prove anything, I guess."

The rumble of an engine starting up vibrated the trailer.

"I thought they didn't work on Sundays?" Mara said, but Levi was already hurrying toward the trailer door to get a better look.

He'd no more pushed it open than the trailer shook, her scream drowned out by the creak of the structure toppling over...

Dana Mentink is a nationally bestselling author. She has been honored to win two Carol Awards, a HOLT Medallion and an RT Reviewers' Choice Best Book Award. She's authored more than thirty novels to date for Love Inspired Suspense and Harlequin Heartwarming. Dana loves feedback from her readers. Contact her at danamentink.com.

Books by Dana Mentink

Love Inspired Suspense

Desert Justice

Framed in Death Valley
Missing in the Desert

True Blue K-9 Unit: Brooklyn

Cold Case Pursuit

True Blue K-9 Unit

Shield of Protection
Act of Valor

Roughwater Ranch Cowboys

Danger on the Ranch
Deadly Christmas Pretense
Cold Case Connection
Secrets Resurfaced

Visit the Author Profile page at Harlequin.com for more titles.

MISSING IN THE DESERT

DANA MENTINK

LOVE INSPIRED SUSPENSE
INSPIRATIONAL ROMANCE

LOVE INSPIRED SUSPENSE

INSPIRATIONAL ROMANCE

ISBN-13: 978-1-335-72252-2

Recycling programs
for this product may
not exist in your area.

Missing in the Desert

Love Inspired
22 Adelaide St. West, 40th Floor
Toronto, Ontario M5H 4E3, Canada
www.Harlequin.com

Printed in U.S.A.

What shall we then say to these things?
If God be for us, who can be against us?
—*Romans* 8:31

To Leona, my walking buddy and tech guru.
Your golden heart makes this world a better place.

ONE

Levi Duke let the engine idle and rubbed his temple. Another headache, courtesy of the wreck. The headaches were probably temporary, the doctors said. He sighed. Yes, the car accident four months before had left him with a scar, but worse yet, his hospital time made him miss out on a perfect horse to add to his herd. That was the real pain of it.

"Not this time," he said. "We're gonna have ourselves a new mare, 'Jo."

Banjo, the sizable mutt with a chunk missing from one ear, sprawled in his passenger seat and licked the knee of Levi's jeans. The dog slithered his way under Levi's palm until he got the ear rub he was looking for. Mission accomplished, he flopped over and presented his belly, long legs taking up more than his fair share of the room. His fleas and the mud were gone now, thanks to a bath that had been a struggle of epic proportions, his leg wound treated, too. His ribs were not quite as prominent as the day Levi had found him panting and half-dead in a dry creek bed. The dog had introduced himself with eyes desperate for help and the faintest of tail wags. Who could say no to that?

The cell phone chimed.

"We're just driving past the Funeral Mountains." Mara's voice was cool, in spite of the faint Southern drawl. Never could hide her feelings. She was upset with him for inviting her brother, Seth, to partner with him in purchasing the Rocking Horse Ranch. Maybe she had a right to be. A busted-up old ranch just outside Death Valley National Park, a place so hot it was nearly uninhabitable four months of the year? Not exactly a surefire moneymaker. But it wasn't really about the money—not for him, anyway. He was surprised Mara had even agreed to accompany Seth to meet the mare. Maybe Mara was softening to the idea? Not likely.

"Be careful," he said. "Road's steep. I'll meet you at the farm and introduce you to Cookie. She's a sweetheart." Offered for sale by a local, the mare would be a perfect fit for their current herd of eleven if co-owner Seth approved. They needed more horses pronto to meet the tourist demands for the November Camp Town Days Festival the following week.

There was a pause. "All right."

He forced cheer into his voice to counter-act her lack of enthusiasm. "Laney and Beckett are having a barbecue at the Hotsprings. They asked me to invite you both." His cousin Beckett's hotel was making a slow recovery after the set of killings that had resulted in Beckett's false imprisonment and a threat to Laney's life. It was easier to forget those days now, as the couple prepared for the spring birth of their first child.

Mara queried her brother and returned her attention to the phone. "Seth says he'd love to go, but I have some business to work on."

Business? Mara helped run her parents' furniture store in Henderson, Nevada, some two hundred miles away. Odd that she'd have business here in podunk Furnace Falls. It wasn't his nature to pry. Then again, she might just be making an excuse to stay far away from him. He blew out a silent breath. Horses were so much easier to read than people, especially women, most especially Mara Castillo.

The pause lingered as he tried to figure out what to say next. The shiver went through him, that strange combination of fascination and bewilderment that raven-haired Mara awakened in him ever since he'd met her in high-school keyboarding class. He'd flunked the typing part, but he sure had spent plenty of time wondering what Mara was thinking in that seat in front of him, her hair dark as the nighttime desert sky.

Mara cut through his thoughts. "See you soon, then."

Face to face he would have answered with a silent nod. "Can't wait." Can't wait? *Way to sound like a sappy teen instead of a savvy ranch owner.* He was still fighting with his tongue to dredge up something articulate when she cut him off.

"Be there in a half hour."

He almost smiled at her annoyed tone. Mara had always worn her heart on her sleeve. There was no pretense about her. He'd finally worked up the courage his senior year to ask her to the school dance.

She'd laughed. "I don't want to cram into a gym and listen to loud music and drink watery punch. How about we go fishing instead?"

They had, and Levi had developed an undeniable crush on his best friend's tomboy sister. He blinked, realizing she'd already disconnected. He'd have to do better than that to prove to her he was a competent business partner for her brother. It was a tall order. The saddlery he'd opened after his return to civilian life had gone belly-up, in spite of regular help from Seth when he could get away from his contracting job in Nevada.

Seth would do anything for Levi, even follow him into enlisting when her family needed him most. A breeze blew across Levi's face, carrying the scent of hard-packed earth and sunshine.

November temperatures were the most palatable of the whole year. Death Valley, the hottest location in North America, cooled somewhat in the fall, making it prime tourist season. The town was abuzz with preparations for Camp Town Days which would feature reenactments of the famous 20 Mule Team journeys. The wagon teams would start in town and roll their way across Furnace Falls to a campsite on the outskirts of town where they could stay to enjoy the vendor displays and plenty of old-fashioned fun. Tourists would need horses and guides, tours of the Keane Wonder Mine and wagon rides into Death Valley National Park. He and Seth would be ready to meet the need especially if they could acquire another even-tempered mare to add to the Rocking Horse family.

The miles passed quickly as he drove to Hank's property which was at the bottom of a perilously pitched road. So pitched, in fact, that if they purchased the animal he'd have to ride the mare up to the flat plateau above, since they could not get a trailer down the grade.

Riding the brakes, he made it to the bottom

and parked on the graveled drive that led to Hank's house and barn. A rumble indicated an approaching vehicle, but the sound was too high and thin for a car engine. Banjo stared out the open window, nose twitching, an agitated whine escaping his fleshy lips. A motorcycle, he decided. Someone visiting Hank's farm...but minutes passed without any sign of an approach. He peered upward where the road wound in and out of sight amid the foothills. Weird... Again, unease tightened his stomach.

But there was nothing wrong, nothing at all. He tried to shake off the feeling. Probably just out of sorts because he'd forgotten to eat lunch. Again.

The glove box of his pickup supplied a half-melted granola bar which he ate, window rolled down. He tossed the last bite to Banjo who swallowed it without even chewing.

Levi figured maybe his agitation was born of his eagerness to return to the ranch. It didn't matter what the naysayers said about the Rocking Horse: it was a paradise to him. Every rusted bolt and warped fence post was part of a dream he'd had since he was four years old visiting his uncle's barn. Cookie the mare was just one more step toward the life he was meant to live in the most fantastic place on earth.

Banjo barked. The mysterious motorcyclist? Still Levi could not spot anything. Odd.

He heard the rumble of what had to be Seth's SUV. A glimpse of bright yellow paint proved him right. He shifted at the thought of seeing Mara. Seth was always the genial, happy-go-lucky guy who reminded Levi of his own brother, Austin. His sister was another breed altogether.

As the vehicle made the hairpin turn and began to inch down the slope, Seth stuck an arm out the window and waved. Levi waved back, grinning.

A sound sliced through the afternoon. His body recognized it before his brain did, and he reflexively ducked. A shot.

A hunter? On private property? Shooting what, birds? The thoughts tumbled as he looked wildly for the source. Banjo began to bark in a frantic, throaty cascade. Was it the motorcyclist he'd heard before? He scanned the foothills, trying to quiet the dog.

A second shot followed the first.

Seth's SUV's windshield shattered. It began to slide to the side of the road.

"No," he yelled in horror.

The car was a blur of yellow, the tires squealing as they labored to keep the vehicle upright. Sun glittered off the broken glass as it turned over and rolled again and again.

* * *

Mara was too shocked to scream. A moment before, her brother had finally been opening up about what had happened with his fiancée.

"Tanya made it clear, sis. She found another guy. Funny thing is, I still love her, you know? I want a fresh start, a new way of living. I can have that on the ranch."

The reply was still on her lips when something punched through the front window, raining chips of glass on her lap. At first she thought it might have been a rock. But how was that possible? A second missile followed, moments later. She felt Seth recoil. Had he been struck?

Out the spidered front window, she saw a man in profile, hat pulled down over his eyes, black bandanna covering his nose and mouth, a long wisp of beard trailing as he lowered a rifle. Then he stepped back into the scrub and disappeared.

"Seth—" she started, breaking off in horror as she saw the blood blooming on his shoulder, his neck, in his hair. He slumped over.

Now the scream did emerge. "Seth!"

He didn't answer, hands falling from the wheel. They began to careen downslope. Bright flashes of sunlight blinded her. Branches crackled as the vehicle plowed off the road into the scrub. She tried to brace herself against the dashboard with one hand and grab Seth's arm to steady him, but the violent juddering tossed them like tumbleweeds. They would have been ejected through the fractured window if not for their seat belts.

A branch thrust through the side window, cutting into her neck. She shrank back before it sliced any deeper toward her carotid.

She thought she might have heard her brother groan. He was alive, he would be okay, she told herself. Again she tried to lean toward him, desperate and terrified, but she could not steady herself against the violent jostling. They bounced off a half-buried boulder sticking up from the ground. The impact set them on a new trajectory.

With a sudden jerk, the SUV flipped on its side. They could not continue their acceleration much longer. She knew the road bottomed out at the farm. Levi would be there, he'd probably already called for help. The car slowed, grinding over the gravel with a tortured squeal that left her teeth on edge.

The movement continued to ease off. She was able to catch sight of Levi charging up the slope, long legs flying. He came to an abrupt stop. She could not see his eyes from under the shadow of his cowboy hat but his mouth opened in a cry she could not hear. A hairy dog followed at his heels.

At the same moment, the SUV jounced over

what must have been a ridge of rock and began once again to tumble out of control.

"Hang on," she yelled to Seth. Small rocks and debris rained through the broken windows as they began to pick up speed again. They'd lose momentum soon, wouldn't they? Levi was close. He'd get her brother out, call for an ambulance. It would all be okay.

Her attention was snagged by an object appearing before them. The upthrust arms of a Joshua tree loomed directly in their path. Its prickly trunk was sturdy as if it had been standing there defying the elements since long before she'd been born. She grabbed at the wheel, trying to divert their course. Too late.

She did not even have time to brace herself as the vehicle slammed into the tree with such force the airbags deployed. The breath was driven out of her. She was flung back against the seat. The airbag exploded like a smack to the face. Her vision was filled with white. Stunned, she could only sit there immobilized, struggling to breathe.

Slowly the bag began to deflate, inch by inch. It subsided enough that she could make sense of their situation. The car was on its side, driver's door to the ground, front bumper crumpled against the Joshua tree. She was hanging upside down, tethered by her seat belt.

Panting, she tried to stop her brain from spinning. Dizziness made her feel sick to her stomach. Was she able to move? Was Seth? Was he alive? She jerked a panicked look down. Her long hair hung in a tousled mass around her face. Shoving it back, she reached over. The driver's-side airbag completely hid him until it slowly began to deflate. Inch by inch, moment by moment. She could hardly stand it. Gradually his head came into view.

"Seth?" she whispered.

He was crumpled below her against the driver's-side door, face turned away. The blood dripping from his curly hair filled her with terror. So much blood. Was this real? Was she in the grip of a heinous nightmare? Silently, she prayed as she tried to get hold of his hand. Her own hands were shaking so badly she could not seem to get them to move on command.

"Seth, please answer me. Say something," she whispered.

"Mara." Levi's face swam into view, his navy blue eyes and shock of ginger hair blurred for a moment until she blinked. He scrambled around trying to reach the driver's door to no avail. The front windshield was a mess of broken glass, rocks and the remnants of the airbags. Instead he climbed up to her passenger door and grunted as he heaved on it. Finally it gave way with a squeak of metal.

Another man, white-haired and stout, appeared at a run, probably the property owner. "Emergency is on its way," he said. "They were over the hill at a call. They'll be here in less than five minutes. What should I do?"

The voices faded in and out. A sense of unreality crowded rational thought. This was a bad dream. She would blink and wake up. Her brother would be knocking on her apartment door teasing her about sleeping late.

"If the sun had to wait for you to plug it in, we'd live in darkness," he'd say.

They would go to their parents' furniture store, and he would help with deliveries while she updated the website and assisted her mother on the floor. She would dust the family picture on the front desk, the one that showed the five of them, including Corinne before she'd run away. This was not, could not, be happening.

"Mara," Levi said again, cutting through her fog. "How badly are you hurt? Can you tell me?"

"What?" She blinked again. "I think… I'm okay. But Seth is bleeding."

"I'll help him. I'm afraid to cut you loose in case you have internal injuries."

"Go help Seth," she said as loudly as she could. "Please, Levi."

He pressed her hand and climbed out, crawling around to the driver's side.

"Hey, buddy," she heard Levi say. "It's gonna be all right. Help's coming."

"Is he…?" she croaked.

"He's alive. I just heard him groan."

And that was all she needed to hear. The desert sun grew dim, and a buzzing sounded in her ears. The older man said, "I heard shooting. Is that what caused this?"

The bearded man had shot into their vehicle, twice.

It had not been an accident. He'd intended to kill.

Who was the man who'd fired the shot?

And why?

Levi's body went suddenly taut, and he jerked a look beyond her. Then he threw himself in front of the passenger window just as she heard the sound of another shot embedding itself in the metal.

TWO

Levi realized his error. He'd been so focused on the wreck he hadn't considered that the shooter might not have given up. Feet crashed through the brush upslope. The gunman was looking for a better vantage point. He'd circle around, and there would be nothing in the way to impede him from killing them all. Easy shots, easy kills.

"Stay low and tell the cops the shooter is still active," he shouted to Hank. Hank scrunched down behind a tree and yanked his cell phone out with shaking hands.

Levi could wait no longer. He sprinted to his truck and grabbed the rifle, Banjo at his heels. He stopped only long enough to steady the weapon before he let loose with a couple of rounds. He didn't have much hope of hitting his target, but he prayed it would be enough to scare the guy off. It only took two rifle shots before he heard the revving of the motorcycle engine. The shooter was going to get away, but there were other priorities right now.

He returned to the wreck and dropped on his knees next to the broken-out driver's-side window fighting a feeling of helplessness. Everything in him wanted to wrestle Seth and Mara free from the ravaged SUV and tend to their wounds. He didn't have a ton of knowledge about medical things, but he knew enough to worry about spinal-cord injuries. If he left them there… What if they were bleeding internally? Dying slowly from invisible wounds?

He used his boot to push aside some of the broken glass and reached inside. Seth was completely unresponsive. He searched for a pulse in his wrist and found one, his fingers coming away sticky with blood. He let out a shuddering breath.

"Mara." There was no reply. "Can you hear me?"

She was quiet, eyes closed, suspended there as if she was drifting. "Stay with me, okay?" he said loudly. "Talk to me." She didn't move. Panic crackled through his nerves. "I know you're mad that Seth bought into the Rocking Horse. Why don't you tell me off? You've been wanting to give me a piece of your mind. Now's the time to let me have it."

Nothing. Goose bumps prickled his skin. He spoke louder.

"You think it's financial suicide, right?" His heart thundered as he both sought out the faint rise and fall of Seth's chest and peered across the ruined front seat at Mara. Banjo raced around to her side of the car, whining and licking at her face.

"That's right, 'Jo," he said. "Wake her up."

Hank crept close, breathing hard. "Shooter took off. How can I help?"

"Stay with Seth and monitor his pulse and breathing."

Hank's eyes widened. "What do I do if they stop?"

"We go to plan B."

"What's that?"

Levi left that question unanswered as he crawled back up the sideways vehicle to check on Mara. The faint warble of a siren echoed down the canyon. To Levi, it was a sound sweeter than his sister's guitar music.

"Hey," he said, easing Banjo away. He gently pulled aside the silky dark curtain of hair and stroked her cheek. "Wake up, Marbles." The nickname had been given her by Corinne, her younger sister. It had always infuriated Mara, and even Seth only dared use it sparingly. He sought her hand, relieved beyond words when she returned his squeeze with a weak flutter of her fingers.

Thank you, God.

He could see where one of the bullets had embedded itself in the roof of the car. The second had not missed.

"Hank," he called. "Did you get a look at the shooter?"

"Not a good one. Male."

"A man? You sure?"

He shrugged. "Not positive."

The sirens echoed loudly now as an ambulance and Inyo County police vehicle made their way down the steep slope. A second ambulance trailed them. Levi's cousin, Sheriff Jude Duke, arrived a minute after the ambulances, leaping out and running to the wreck.

"What happened?" he demanded, mouth tight, standing aside as the volunteer firefighters and paramedics began their work. Another squad car arrived, and a second officer got out to assist.

Levi shook his head. "Someone shot at them."

Jude did a double take. "What?"

He told his cousin about the motorcycle noise. Hank added his own details to the story.

Jude's gaze was sharp. "Why would someone do that? No hunting around here. Mara and Seth weren't trespassing on anyone's property. They haven't even lived in town for decades."

Levi stared at the wreck. "Question of the hour." Who? Why?

Jude pulled out his cell phone. "Is Mara conscious?"

"Not enough to tell me anything."

"Why were Seth and Mara coming here?"

Because of me, he thought miserably. No doubt Mara was representing the Castillo family in trying to get Seth to back out of the ranch partnership before the paperwork was finalized. He told Jude about the ranch, their arrangement to see the mare. "It was supposed to be just Seth, but he said Mara insisted on coming. Beckett and Laney invited us to the Hotsprings for dinner, but she said she had some kind of business in town."

Together, they helped clear the front windshield so the medics could free Seth. A wad of gauze collected the blood that flowed from his forehead as they immobilized his neck and spine and loaded him into the ambulance.

Seth was completely limp. Levi ground his teeth together to keep from groaning. His best friend, a guy who would give you his shirt and the shoes to go with it… They'd gone through the last three years of high school together and basic training before they were dispatched into different army specialties, Levi a mechanic and Seth a medical corpsman. Seth was universally liked. He had the same magnetic, good-guy persona as Levi's brother Austin that made people gravitate to him.

No one wanted to hurt Seth, except maybe for the woman who'd cheated on him, Tanya, the one he'd meant to marry. But she wouldn't have had anything to do with this…would she? What would she have to gain by hiring someone to shoot him?

The second ambulance pulled closer, assisting as they took the same head and neck precautions with Mara. She opened her eyes once, terror written in their black depths. He edged close and stroked her forearm. "It's going to be okay. They're taking you and Seth to the hospital. I'll be right behind you."

He was not sure his words were any comfort. His own stomach was leapfrogging at the sight of the wrecked car, saturated with blood. The what-ifs loomed large.

It took Jude's tap on his shoulder to make him realize he was being spoken to.

"Are you okay to drive? They'll triage at the clinic and most likely chopper them to Las Vegas."

Las Vegas, where the trauma center was equipped for their level of injuries.

"Yes. I can drive. I'll drop Banjo at the ranch first. Should I—" he swallowed a lump "—call their folks? They run a furniture store in Henderson."

"I remember them being a close family."

He nodded. "They'll want to be there."

"Why don't I contact them? You get on the road." Jude paused. "I'll call the Hotsprings, and fill Beckett in, too."

Levi hardly heard. He was jogging to his car with one desire overriding anything else. *Get to the hospital. Get to Seth and Mara.*

Mara did not know how much time had passed before she swam back to consciousness with a start. A nurse was peering into her eyes. "Welcome back, Ms. Castillo. I'm Deb, and you're at Las Vegas Memorial. You've had an accident, but fortunately your injuries are minor."

"Injuries?" Mara croaked. Fear nibbled at the edges of her mind, but she was still swimming through a mental fog.

"You have a mild concussion and a sprained wrist, along with some lacerations to your shoulder and neck, which we sutured," the nurse explained. "Nothing that won't mend with time. You're going to be A-OK."

She did not feel remotely okay. Her head was hammering, and her wrist was on fire. It was another long, fuzzy moment until the worry circling in her unconscious mind burst to flame.

"Seth," she cried, jerking to a sitting position. "How is my brother?" The nurse pushed her back down on the bed.

"He is being taken care of."

She sucked in gulps of air as she recalled their tumbling slide and the blood, so much blood. "Is he okay?"

The nurse's expression did not give anything away. "I will have the doctor come talk to you."

"Please…can't you tell me anything?"

The nurse had a professional, soothing response. "I promise the doctor treating your brother will come and fill you in as soon as she can."

Maddening. "I have to know. Just tell me…"

But the nurse patted her arm and strode to the door, leaving her alone. Why wouldn't they tell her? What if…? Tears filled her eyes. What if he didn't make it? Her brother was her champion, her hero. He was the only one who knew everything about what happened before her sister ran away, and never once had he been anything but supportive.

"She made her choices, Mara. Don't let what she did color your whole life."

"I haven't."

"No? What happened to your plans to be a vet tech?"

"Someone has to help Mom and Dad run the store."

"That someone doesn't have to be you, and they've told you as much. Let go of your guilt."

Remembering his crooked grin made muscles tighten in her chest, and it suddenly became difficult to breathe. In the ruined SUV he'd been so still. What if those terrible moments were their last together? Seth might be ripped from her life, just like Corinne. She began to tremble.

The door opened and Levi entered, holding his cowboy hat clutched in his fist. Her breath came in tortured spurts. He made it to her bedside in two strides of his long legs and took her hands in his. He didn't say anything at first, just gripped her fingers.

"Breathe slowly."

She did. When the tightness in her lungs subsided, she swallowed. Part of her dreaded asking, but she had to know.

"Is Seth alive?" she whispered.

"Yes."

Alive. She closed her eyes, and then an ocean of tears let loose. All she could do was sob and squeeze his hands. He held on, a silent comfort, though she didn't want him to be. Eventually, she let go and took the box of tissues he offered. "Thank you. I didn't mean to fall apart."

Levi did not say anything, true to form.

She was about to press him for more details about Seth when the doctor came in.

"I'm Dr. Imani Rice," she said, settling into a chair, "a surgeon here at Las Vegas Memorial." She looked impossibly young to be a surgeon. "I operated on your brother. He was injured by a bullet that skimmed his cheekbone and struck his right temple. Fortunately, it appears to have ricocheted off something in the car instead of striking him directly."

Mara gulped in a breath. It wasn't a nightmare. Her brother had been shot. Her heart beat so loud it almost drowned out the doctor.

"He came through the surgery, and his vitals are steady at the moment."

Steady. She wanted to rejoice, but she sensed there was something more.

"He's in a coma," she heard the doctor add.

A coma? Cold sweat broke out on Mara's forehead. "When will he come out of it?"

The doctor clicked her pen closed. "We're going to do everything we can to make that happen."

Now all her alarm bells were shrilling. "Is there a chance he won't?"

"His brain has sustained a significant injury and there is considerable swelling. We removed a hematoma to alleviate the pressure, but the first twenty-four hours are often unpredictable with injuries of this nature. We will know more as time goes by. I promise I will keep you informed. Will there be any more family here to keep in the loop?"

Mara closed her eyes. Her mother and father would be crushed. Having endured the disappearance of their youngest daughter, how would they cope with the current situation? She balled her hands into fists. They would survive because they knew God was with them in their suffering, every moment. But surviving and living were two completely different things. She was grateful when Levi answered the doctor for her.

"Her parents are on their way."

When Mara reopened her eyes, there was an Inyo County sheriff standing behind the doctor and another tapping a message into a cell phone. She recognized the tallest as Jude Duke. She'd known him casually in high school, since Seth was close with the Dukes. The doctor excused herself, and Mara forced herself to focus on Jude.

"How are you feeling, Ms. Castillo?"

"Mara, please. I'm not sure even how to describe how I am. A wreck, I think. My mom…"

He nodded. "Your parents should be here in a couple of hours."

She sank down deeper into the bed. Tears threatened again. As much as she wanted to compose herself and talk to the officer, she could not get her emotions in check. Sniffling, she tried to speak and then stopped. Each word stumbled over her tongue and refused to emerge. All she could think about was Seth lying in a coma from which he might not awaken.

Levi shot a look at Jude. "It's not… I mean could your questions wait a little while?"

Jude started to answer when his phone rang. "We'll come back after I check in with the other officers. I'm very sorry about the accident."

After the sheriff and the officer left, Levi poured her a glass of water. She sipped, grateful that he wasn't peppering her with questions. He sat in the chair, forearms on his knees, and scrubbed a hand through his hair. His silent ways had always faintly annoyed her. At their family gatherings in Furnace Falls all those years ago, she would sometimes forget he was there, he would remain so quiet as the chatter filled up the corners of the house.

"Don't you talk?" she'd teased.

"Only when I have something to say."

Now she found herself grateful for his reticence. The last thing she needed right now was small talk or empty platitudes about everything turning out all right.

She watched him and thought about Seth. Best friends, Seth would do anything for Levi, even ruin himself financially on a wreck of a ranch. Levi knew that Seth had always wanted to live away from the city, closer to a country existence rather than the bustling Nevada city where he worked as a contractor. All Levi had to do was mention he was looking for a partner in his sad-sack ranch. Seth would not have said no to a friend, especially Levi, even after the guy had already failed in one business endeavor. Now her brother was unresponsive. Did he understand somewhere deep down what was happening to him? Was he scared?

"None of this should have happened. I wish we'd never come here," she blurted, suddenly furious.

He jerked a look at her. "I don't know what to say."

"There's nothing you can say, is there? Seth and I came back here because my brother would do anything for you, including investing in your ranch."

"I didn't twist his arm. He was eager to partner up."

"Because you are his friend and he was vulnerable after Tanya dumped him. You took advantage."

He flinched as if she'd struck him. "He's my best friend."

As if that excused anything. "Mine, too, and

now he might not make it." She blinked back angry tears. When her vision cleared, she saw Levi standing now, hat dangling uselessly from his fingers, and there was such a pool of sorrow in his gaze that her anger dissipated into guilt.

"I apologize," she gulped. "My emotions are all over the place. You weren't the cause of the accident." Accident? Hardly. The bearded man knew exactly what he was doing. He was directly responsible, not Levi. "I caught a glimpse of the man who shot at us. He stepped out from behind a rock with his rifle aimed. He had a long wispy beard with a brown felt hat pulled low and a black bandanna covering his face."

Levi gaped. "That's good. We can give that description to Jude when he comes back."

"But why would anybody…?" She felt her windpipe constricting again. She wrapped her arms around herself and squeezed to keep her wits from flying in all different directions or hurling her desperation at Levi.

He bent, his gaze riveting her eyes to his. He said it so softly it was almost a whisper. "How can I help?"

"You can't."

"I'll stay. If you need anything…"

"My parents will be here soon." The words would hardly come out.

"I'll be here until then. I can wait outside if you want."

What did she want? She wanted her brother to live, to be okay, to wake up with his customary ebullience in place. She wanted him to come marching in the door and help himself to a glass of her fresh-squeezed lemonade and pronounce it *finer than frog feathers*. She desperately wanted what had happened to be a terrible dream she'd awaken from any moment.

He's in a coma.

Fear threatened to swallow her up. "I want to pray."

Her voice was no more than a tiny murmur in the sterile room.

He paused for a beat, knelt on the floor, closed his eyes and began to pray, softly, rhythmically, like soothing music. Slowly her eyes closed, and she let the horror of the day fade into sleep.

THREE

Jude returned to interview Mara while the nurse was checking on her. Levi stepped outside to allow them privacy. He tried to ignore the scent of antiseptic and the unnatural hush that reminded him all too clearly of his stay in this same hospital after his accident. But this was far worse now, because he was on the other end, consumed by fear about Seth's prognosis.

In the waiting room he found his cousin Beckett and brother Austin.

Beckett stood and clapped Levi on the back. "Glad you're okay. And Mara, too."

Austin, all six foot six muscled bulk of him, was not as restrained. He grabbed Levi up in a bone-crushing hug that reminded him of their teen wrestling matches. He knew it cost Austin some pain, since he'd wrecked his shoulder in a climbing accident. "Aww, man. I can't believe it," he said. "Who would shoot at Seth?"

"Mara got a look at the guy." He repeated her

description. "Sound like anybody we know in town?"

Austin huffed. "Describes just about everyone involved in the reenactment stuff."

Levi sighed. His brother was right. Dozens of people were arriving in Furnace Falls and nearby Beatty to participate in the historical reenactment of the 20 Mule Teams that had transported Borax from the valley floor to higher elevations. They were all going for that so-called old-sourdough look.

Beckett rubbed a hand over his clean-shaven chin. "Can you tell us anything else?"

They discussed all the details Levi could remember, but none added any clarity to the situation.

Jude emerged from Mara's room, frowning.

"Learn something helpful?" Levi asked.

"The meeting she was supposed to have tonight was at J and K Excavators here in town."

Levi quirked an eyebrow. "Excavators? What for?"

"I think you should have her tell you about that in person. I am going to speak with them tomorrow. Her parents didn't know anything about it. Did Seth happen to mention it?"

"No, we were focused on the horses. We talked about having some land cleared for a new corral, but we didn't get into specifics."

"Maybe Mara was going to do the legwork to surprise you and Seth?" Jude suggested.

He sighed. "No. Mara and her parents didn't want Seth investing in the ranch in the first place."

Jude's eyebrow shot up. "Ah. Awkward." He detached his keys from his belt. "The excavating business is probably unrelated to what happened. Worth a check, though." He left Levi to his tumultuous thoughts.

The late afternoon passed slowly. A blur of doctors and nurses paraded in and out of Mara's room. Levi insisted Beckett return home. Beckett's relief at the idea was clear. He loathed to be away from Laney even for a short while. After what had almost happened to her the month before, he didn't blame his cousin. The whole debacle had been horrendous, but it had left Beckett with an awareness of how utterly precious and perilous life could be.

Austin stayed, and their sister Willow arrived, comforting as best she could with rapid-fire conversation and dozens of tearful hugs until she had to leave to escort a photography tour into the park.

He was able to check on Mara a few times but found her dozing. His questions about her business appointment would have to wait. The hours crawled by. He paced the hallways trying and failing to make some sense of what had happened. Austin fielded the calls from various friends who had heard of the accident. Levi was grateful not to have to talk to anyone.

Fred and Diane Castillo arrived in the early evening. Levi offered Fred a handshake and accepted a tearful hug from his wife before they hurried into Mara's room. Levi continued his pacing, trying to keep his mind off the anguish that was no doubt being shared by the family.

The Castillos split their time between Mara's hospital room and Seth's. When they had news, they shared it with Levi, though it was meager. Seth remained comatose, which was not unexpected. It could take days or weeks before the swelling abated and they could ascertain the extent of the damage.

"We're going to get a hotel room here in town for as long as we need to," Fred said.

"Yes, sir. Mara, too?"

Fred shot him a look that was somewhere between pain and chagrin. "She's got other plans. I'll let her tell you about them."

Other plans? He couldn't imagine her leaving town with Seth in such a condition.

He led his wife toward the exit, though she resisted at first. "We need a couple of hours of sleep, honey. The doctor will call us if there's a development," he pressed.

"If there's anything I can do, please let me know," Levi said.

Fred turned back before he followed her. "As a matter of fact, there is. Seth invested everything he had into your ranch against my advice. Ever since you two were high schoolers, he would have done anything for you, including joining the military which we were against as well. Your saddlery failed, right? Seth told me you lost everything in that bankruptcy. Do what you can to make sure he didn't throw everything away by trusting you with this ranch scheme."

Levi was left staring, mouth open as they departed.

Austin blew out a breath. "That was harsh, but he's in a bad way right now. Don't take it to heart. You didn't coerce Seth."

Levi shook his head. "He's right, though. I gotta get the Rocking Horse into the black. It's all I can do for Seth right now." He eyed his brother. "Can you tend to the horses tonight? I'll drive back as soon as I can." Austin ran a carpentry shop in town when he wasn't adventuring around the globe in his small plane, but they'd both grown up with horses. He was as comfortable with tending them as Levi was. Levi would not insult him by asking if it would be too much strain on his shoulder. His brother's pride had already taken a beating when his fiancée left him at the altar.

Austin nodded. "No sweat. On my way."

"Oh, and there's a dog. I call him Banjo. He crawled under my truck a couple of weeks ago. He takes his guard duties seriously, and he's iffy about men, so let him check you out before you charge in, okay?"

"I'll give him a treat," he said. "Buy him off with bacon or something."

"Careful. Too many treats and he upchucks. Give him some kibble from the cupboard."

Austin shook his head. "Are you running a ranch or a homeless animal rescue?"

"Sometimes I can't decide."

After a thumbs-up, Austin left.

He stared at the closed door of Mara's hospital room. If Mara didn't intend to stay in Las Vegas with her parents, what could she have decided?

He felt an overwhelming urge to return to the Rocking Horse, to press forward with their plans to showcase the ranch in the Camp Town Days. If he couldn't...the place really would go bust, and he'd have let the Castillo family down in a big way.

Guilt flickered in his gut.

If he hadn't sought Seth out to invest...

If he hadn't invited him to come meet the mare...

He sucked in a breath. God didn't want him to paralyze himself with guilt. Action was what was needed. He would do everything in his power to keep the ranch alive and pray with all his might that Seth would awaken.

Mara tried to block out the pain the next morning. Every muscle screamed its displeasure. She'd parried her parents' apprehension with a calm she did not entirely feel.

"It's the best thing. The Rocking Horse Ranch needs to succeed," she'd said firmly. And it was the only thing she could do for her brother. She'd already bummed a pencil from a nurse and been scribbling down a list of ranch-related questions.

A knuckle rap on the door announced Levi's arrival. His chin was dark with a five-o'clock shadow, and he still wore the same jeans and T-shirt. Clearly he'd stayed all night. Her cheeks went hot, remembering how he'd knelt and prayed at her bedside. So he had a sweet side… It definitely did not excuse him from roping her poor brother into a business disaster. Seth was an easy touch, and Levi knew it.

"Morning," he said. "I heard you were being discharged."

"I thought you were leaving, since my parents showed up."

He hoisted a shoulder. "Your dad said you had a plan. Figured maybe I could help."

She nodded and took a breath. Might as well get it out quickly. "There's a cabin on the Rocking Horse in addition to the main house, right? Where Seth was going to stay?"

He nodded. "More of a shack, really. Seth moved some of his stuff in already."

"I want to stay there."

His brows shot nearly to his hairline. "What?"

"I'm going to split my time between the hospital and the ranch. I'm helping you through Camp Town Days."

His jaw dropped. "That's…surprising."

She held up her chin, expecting him to try and talk her out of it. "It's for the best."

He was quiet for a moment longer. "What about your business in town?"

She froze. The change of subject surprised her. "It's no big deal."

"Why were you going to visit J and K Excavation? Jude told me."

She wanted to be angry, to tell him off with a *it's none of your business*. Instead she chewed her lower lip and gave him the truth. "It's nothing. Probably just a waste of time anyway. Something to do with my sister."

"Corinne? But I thought she was…"

"Presumed dead almost five years ago when

she was sixteen. Yes, that's the general consensus. The police investigated and figured she was despondent about a boy and ran off into Death Valley Park and either got lost or fell and never made her way out. A ranger found her shoe on a steep trail."

"I remember Seth telling me he got leave from the army to return home for the funeral. He never really wanted to talk about it with me."

She nodded. "I believe that's what happened, always have. It's just that I got a strange text a week ago. One word, *Marbles*, with a capital *M*."

Now a furrow formed between his brows. "Your nickname?"

"I called the number where the text originated, and it belonged to the excavation company here in Furnace Falls. It's the owner's cell phone number, a man named Jerry, and he had no idea how that text was sent to me."

Levi seemed deep in thought as she continued.

"Anyway, Jerry was kind. He told me what job sites he'd been at where someone might have used his phone, because he leaves it in his truck sometimes, but he's lost the phone. He said I was welcome to come talk to him." She plucked at the blanket. "It seemed like the time to do it, since I was coming to check out the ranch, anyway. I didn't tell Seth. I didn't want to upset him or have him think I was imagining things because of guilt."

"Why would you feel guilty about what Corinne did?"

No way did she want to unpack that mess at the moment, especially not with Levi. She looked away. "Not important."

"Receive any more messages from that number?"

"No." She heard the hesitation in her own voice. Time to come clean. "About four months ago, I got this postcard mailed to our home. The address was written in crayon. There was no message, but it was postmarked in Death Valley. Weird, huh? I figured it was a mistake, meant for someone else, but it was strange."

"Very."

None of this matters, anyway, now that Seth's been hurt. I need to make him my focus."

Something sharpened in Levi's gaze. He frowned.

"What is it?"

He was silent for a full minute. She was just about to ask him again, when he started speaking. "Last summer when Seth visited me, he drove your car, remember? Because he wanted me to check the engine, but I got into a wreck…"

She nodded to keep him talking. "How could I forget? My car was totaled."

He paused. "The driver in front of me slammed on their brakes, and I went into a culvert. It was written up as a hit-and-run. I was real foggy, but I had the vaguest sense someone climbed down and looked inside the wreck. All this time I figured it was my brain playing tricks on me."

She stared, muscles tightening in her stomach. "Levi, what are you getting at?"

"The shooter yesterday hit Seth, but he could just as easily have been aiming for you."

Now she could only stare at him as his meaning slowly dawned.

"Think about it, Mara. I was driving your car last summer, and someone caused a wreck. Fast-forward to you and Seth, both in the front seat of his SUV, sitting inches apart. What if he wasn't the target?"

Levi's wreck and the one that almost killed Seth were related? Both were attempts to kill… neither Levi nor her brother? Her throat felt sand-dry. "I don't have any enemies."

He shook his head. "I don't mean to scare you, but you can't know that for sure. The two incidents mean something, Mara. And now, there's another problem," he said slowly. "You got a look at the shooter. You can identify him."

"I didn't see him… Well, only a glance, and I didn't recognize him."

"He doesn't know that."

Her mouth went dry.

"We'd better talk to Jude right away."

She could only shake her head. Levi must be wrong, connecting dots that weren't there. But if he was right...then, someone wanted her dead.

Someone with a wispy beard and a brown felt hat.

"I'll call him," he said. "My phone is dead so I'll grab my charger from the truck and come right back. Okay?"

She nodded. Her head was throbbing, and her stomach churned. Murder. Who would want to murder her? She managed a furniture store, lived a quiet life. Levi must be imagining things. But she couldn't conceive of anyone targeting Seth, either.

Tanya. Had Seth taken out a life-insurance policy and named his soon-to-be-wife a beneficiary? Could Levi's whole theory about her being the target be wrong? Her eyes burned and she closed them, trying to push away the chaos in her mind.

Rest, that's what she needed. A nap.

Closing her eyes, she sank gratefully toward sleep. A shadow flickered against her eyelids. A dream, it must be. She could not summon up the energy even to open her eyes.

A whisper of movement fanned the hairs along her arms.

As the edge of unconsciousness finally crept across her senses, she forced herself to respond. Her eyes flew open.

A man stood at her bedside, a ski mask over his face, the mouth hole not quite concealing the whiskers curling out from underneath. Her scream was cut off as he shoved a gloved hand over her lips.

He knelt close, so close his breath smelled sour, felt hot on her cheek.

"Why aren't you dead?" he whispered.

Fear clawed at her stomach as she tried to pry away his fingers. They were like iron bands, pressing into her cheeks. Fumbling next to her, she sought something, anything with which to fend him off.

Her frantic grasp found nothing except a pencil.

Snatching it up, she stabbed as hard as she could.

FOUR

Levi was at the end of the corridor when Mara's door opened. A man in a ski mask ran out on the heels of her scream.

"Stop!" he thundered, but the guy was already slamming through the exit door at the end of the hall. An orderly pushing a cart of folded linens shot a startled look at the intruder. "Call security to stop that man!" Levi plowed into Mara's room. Terror licked at every nerve. Was he too late?

She was kneeling on the bed, hands clutched around the sheets.

He ran to her. "Did he hurt you?"

She was breathing too hard to answer at first. He gripped her forearm and waited. After a moment she answered. "He was the one who got hurt. I stabbed him with a pencil, and he let go long enough for me to scream. He ran out with my pencil still stuck in his bicep."

Levi could not hide his smile of admiration. "Well done."

Slowly those marvelous dark-chocolate eyes swiveled to his. "Even though he wore a ski mask, I could tell it was the same person who shot at us. Same build, and I could see bits of his wispy beard poking through the mouth hole. He asked me why I wasn't dead." She gulped, and he captured her quaking hands in his. "He…he tried to kill me. Again." Her voice cracked.

Never in his life had Levi wished so hard that he was wrong. "I shouldn't have left you. I thought you were safe in the hospital. Dumb on my part."

Two nurses hurried in along with a security guard.

The guard said "Police are on their way. Lobby security didn't catch him. He made it out of the building."

Levi heard Mara's groan of defeat. "We've got some help this time," he said. "There are cameras in the halls and stairwells. They captured him, I'm sure."

The guard nodded. "Yep. His face was covered, but we got him on film."

When the local police arrived, Mara explained in detail what had happened. They arranged for hospital security to post a guard at her door, which eased Levi's mind.

When the police left, Jude called and Levi put the phone on speaker. "I got the rundown. How are you, Mara?"

"Okay. Please don't mention this to my parents," she pleaded. "I told the local police the same. They have enough on their hands with Seth."

"I understand," Jude said. "The doctors say you'll be released tomorrow. With hospital staff alerted, I'd say you'll be safe as a bug in a rug until they let you loose."

"About that," Levi said, straightening his shoulders for courage. "You should go home. Back to Henderson."

Mara lifted her chin, and a glint in her eyes shone indicating she was ready for battle. "Not until Seth is well enough to be transferred and my parents have left."

Levi appealed to Jude. "I'm right, aren't I, Jude? Some guy has tried to kill her twice since she hit town. Furnace Falls isn't a safe place for her."

There was a moment's hesitation. "I've already spoken to her about that, and I don't believe I changed her mind on the point. Another option would be for her to stay in a hotel in Las Vegas, but if this guy is bent on killing her, it wouldn't take him long to track her down. Not hard to get into a hotel room. Easier than a hospital, in fact."

Mara nodded her agreement.

Jude continued. "If she's bent on staying close, I'd say she's safer on the ranch with you, Levi, and that annoying mountain of a dog you've taken in. He still doesn't trust me, even though I gave him part of my cheeseburger last time. Plus you've got Austin, Beckett and Willow close by, and they know the ins and outs of Furnace Falls. Lots of eyes, and all three are excellent shots, I might add."

He made one more attempt. "Your parents will want you close to them here in Las Vegas." Even as he said it, he realized the flaw. If Mara was a target, that would make her mom and dad vulnerable also. What else could he say? He was sorting through ideas when Mara stopped him by grasping his wrist. Her fingers were dainty and cool, so soft compared to his calloused, leathery paws.

"Levi, I appreciate your concern, but the fact is everyone I love is here." Tears appeared in her eyes. Her voice broke on the last word. "I promise I won't be stupid and put myself in risky situations. I'm smart, and I'm not reckless." She paused again as if to gather herself. "The only way I can help Seth is to help you, so that's what I am going to do."

Jude cleared his throat tactfully. "I've got a phone conference with the Las Vegas PD right now. Talk to you both later." He disconnected.

Levi hung around as long as he could. The guard was installed, and the police were keeping close tabs on Mara, but he found it was hard to leave.

Finally, she made the decision for him. "Thank you for being here, Levi, but there's no need for you to stay. My parents will drop me at your ranch tomorrow when I'm released."

He felt the sting of it in Mara's words as he said goodbye to her at the hospital. She didn't quite look at him, her gaze roving over the blankets. *Your ranch.* The slight emphasis on the *your* told him exactly what she thought of the Rocking Horse, which rankled him. It was their ranch, his and Seth's. And yeah, it wasn't the slickest property, and there were scant amenities, but it was so much more than the sum total of its dusty acres. Aside from the barn and horse shelters, there were precisely two structures on the property, the main house and the small cabin with a scant hundred fifty feet of dusty land between them. Mara would probably despise it.

Ease up, Levi. Consider what she's just gone through. She'd almost been killed, and her brother might very well not make it. She could identify the would-be assassin, and that might put her life in continued danger. Plenty of stress to go around. And anyway, they both wanted the same thing…for Seth to survive and for the ranch to succeed. God willing, the two things would come to pass.

The landscape morphed into the softly undulating foothills, not the drab brown that people expected, but tones of silver, bronze, gold and burnt orange. Every now and again, a vein of rich green was evident, colored by the decomposition of the mica in the rock, a taste of what visitors flocked to see in Artist's Palette in Death Valley. To his mind, this spot on the globe was blessed with beauty beyond measure—it was just a different kind of beauty than other, less severe landscapes. Still he couldn't help feeling trepidatious about Mara's reaction to the accommodations at the Rocking Horse. It was one thing for Seth to bunk in the old cabin which until recently had been filled with damaged saddles and unused blankets. His own siblings wouldn't stay in such accommodations. Willow rented a house in town, and Austin lived in an apartment above his carpentry shop. Levi lived alone on the ranch, and the amenities seemed sufficient. With Mara staying there…well, that was a horse of a different color altogether.

As he pulled onto the drive that led to Rocking Horse Ranch, he waited for the peace to overtake him. The long stretched-out driveway seemed to beckon him. The horses were meandering contentedly, their water trough full, thanks to Austin, enjoying the milder afternoon sun. Banjo appeared, ears stiff and posture tense, barking up a storm. Levi idled the engine and cranked down the passenger window.

"It's me, 'Jo. Remember?"

Banjo stopped in midbark, and then with a single bound, he vaulted through the open window into the passenger seat and set about slavering every square inch of Levi that he could reach.

"All right," Levi said, pushing away the dangling tongue. "I got it. You were just doing your job." Banjo would be a formidable opponent to anyone sneaking onto the property to harm Mara. "Good boy. You are the newly appointed head of ranch security."

Banjo seemed pleased with his new accolade. He escorted Levi around the property, checking on the horses, especially Fancy, a senior citizen whose eye problem was responding well to treatment. Tomorrow he would empty the trough and refill it with clean, fresh water. Hydration was ultra-important in the ferocious Death Valley climate, even in the cooler months. They continued the endless round of chores interrupted by repeated calls to the hospital until he was assured Mara was resting safely. His query to Jude met with the information that the LVPD was reviewing the video footage, but the man had been masked so identification would be tricky. Thoughts chased each other around his skull until he tumbled into bed.

The next afternoon just after one, his sister Willow drove up as he was heading to the cabin for a bottle of water and a snack. Her hair glinted in the sunlight like the palest fall leaves, a tamer shade of his own rusty red. She greeted Banjo who, Levi noticed, had only barked twice before he applied his tongue greeting. Women were okay in his doggy brain. She waved with one hand, the other holding a box balanced on her hip. She squeezed Levi in a hug.

"How's Mara?"

"I called again this morning. Quiet night. No problems."

"Are you sure this is a good idea?" she demanded, getting right to the point, as usual. "Should Mara be coming here if she's in danger?"

"No, but I don't think anything short of a platoon of Marines is going to stop her."

Willow cocked her head in that birdlike way. "Really? She was always so quiet in high school."

Still waters, he thought. "She's not a kid anymore." Something about that statement made his stomach tighten. She was no longer the object of his teen infatuation. Nothing little girl about Mara Castillo. They weren't friends…and not exactly enemies. Not romantically connected, for sure. And he didn't think they qualified as partners in business. Or maybe they did. He felt stymied and uncertain.

Willow did not appear to notice his discomfiture as they opened the door of the stifling cabin where Mara would stay. "I cleared off the cot when you called last night, and put fresh linens on it. It didn't help much. It would be better if she stayed in your room at the main house and you bunked here. Your digs aren't much better, but you have paint on the walls, even if it is an ugly shade of beige."

"That's exactly what I thought, but that's another argument I lost." He gazed at the miniscule cabin. At least the roof was sound: he'd fixed that up last winter, and the plumbing worked to supply the tiny bathroom. There was no way to fix the warped wood floor or even to paint the dingy interior before she arrived. He'd have to get a minifridge so she could at least have access to cold bottled water and maybe bring in a little table. It was definitely not the place for a lady. His mother would concur.

Willow offered the box. "Here's the portable

air conditioner you asked me to buy for you. You owe me forty-two dollars."

He sighed. Forty-two dollars that should have gone toward fence repairs. Disregarding the instructions, he put the unit on the floor and fiddled with it until he got it working. "Maybe I can get a rug or something. At least put up some curtains and—"

"Umm… I don't think there's time for that," Willow said, inclining her head in the direction of the window. "Look."

Banjo started up a clamor about the approaching vehicle. Levi gaped at the sight. Jude drove his police car, and Mara sat in the passenger seat.

"How could she be here already?" he said. "The doctors let her go?"

"Maybe she got that platoon of Marines to help convince them." Willow poked his arm, and he realized he was standing there with his mouth open, while Banjo circled the squad car.

Ready or not, his new ranch resident had arrived.

Mara watched the big dog approach Jude on high alert. Jude stayed still until the dog had got a good sniff, tossed him a biscuit and then opened the door for Mara. In a matter of moments, Banjo had approved both Jude and Mara. She put down her bag and crouched with a twinge of pain to rub the dog's ears, fingering the tattered one. "Hello, you handsome animal. You're thin, very thin."

"We're working on that. His name's Banjo," Levi said. "How is Seth?"

"No change for worse, or for better. I left after visiting hours, and Jude was there so he offered me a ride."

"I left a message on your phone telling you we were en route," Jude said.

"Sorry, I lose track when I'm taking care of the horses. Any progress?"

Jude rolled his shoulders, stretching his tall frame. "So far we haven't found any witnesses to the shooting or the hospital attack except the janitor. He's real nearsighted, so I don't think that's going to go anywhere."

"So where does that leave the investigation?"

Jude's radio crackled, and he quieted it with a twist of a knob. "Still looking at the crime scene here in town. There are no prints on the spent cartridges, so we don't have anywhere to go with it at the moment. Hank's niece down the road a piece said she saw a motorcycle headed out of the valley. The driver may or may not have matched the description Mara provided."

"I'm still not convinced she'll be safe here," Levi said.

Mara straightened. "Don't talk as if I'm not

here. We've been through this. Until my brother is okay to be transferred, I'm not leaving, and neither are my parents."

"This is the best option at the moment," Jude said, eyeing Banjo who was sitting with tail wagging as if he was involved in the discussion. "Keep it quiet that she's staying on the ranch. I'll have an officer drive the area twice a day just to be sure, but it's easy to spot a stranger here, and since she's insisting on helping out with the ranch—"

"But—" Levi said.

"Insisting," Mara said firmly. "I'm subbing in just to get through the Camp Town Days. It's the only way to save this place."

Levi's sharpened look told her she'd not been wise in using the phrase *this place*. She would have to work harder to keep her emotions in check. There was nothing to be gained by being at loggerheads when they were trying to save the ranch her brother had staked his future on.

Willow checked her phone. "Gotta go. I'm taking some publicity pictures." She gave Mara a curt nod. Was it Mara's imagination, or was there a brusque quality to Willow's voice? She was protective of her brother, no doubt. That they had in common. "Talk to you later, Levi," she said more warmly.

"I'll be leaving, too," said Jude. "Text me anytime." He handed Mara's bag to Levi. Jude followed Willow down the long drive.

Mara swallowed back a swell of nerves at being left alone on a dilapidated ranch with Levi Duke. *Just for a few weeks, for Seth.*

Levi opened the door of the cabin for Mara. "I'm sorry, it's not much. I really think you'd be more comfortable in the main house. I…"

Mara walked past him and took it all in, the tiny room, the sliver of a bathroom, piled boxes in the corner, the one and only picture on the wall, a black-and-white photo with a crooked frame showing the ranch in earlier days. It was hot and stuffy. Sweat prickled her neck. "It's completely fine."

"I'll hook up the air conditioner, but really, I—"

She turned. "Levi, quit fussing. I don't require much. I invited myself here, and I didn't expect it to be the Ritz." Her gaze raked the neatly made cot and hand-sewn quilt. "And for now, it makes me feel closer to my brother to be here." An unexpected lump formed in her throat.

That stopped him from whatever he'd been about to say. He touched her shoulder, and she bowed her head, emotion rolling through her body like a storm across the desert.

"I can't tell you how sorry I am that this happened, Mara."

She shuddered and then pulled away, reinserting the distance between them. "He'll get better. In the meantime, I'm going to do what I can here."

"You don't have to. I can handle it."

She straightened. "There's a meeting tomorrow, if I've got the details correct. It's a planning session to work out the details about the Rocking Horse's participation in Camp Town Days, right?"

"Yes, along with the vendors and the mule-team relay. Lots of people will be there."

"I'll be ready."

"Lots of people means that whoever took a shot at you could sneak in, too."

"As Jude said, I'm as safe here as anywhere, and I don't intend to go wandering around on my own. I'm stubborn, but I'm not stupid."

"I know. I remember when you tried to help me with an algebra test."

She'd had a suspicion back then that he hadn't cared much about the outcome of the test, but he had enjoyed Mara's tutoring instruction. He would bring a bunch of peaches pilfered from his mother's fruit bowl as a study snack. Fruit had never tasted as delicious before or since.

"You should have gotten an A."

He smiled. "Trust me. I was happy as a lark with the B."

She laughed and for a moment, it lifted her spirits. "That was a long time ago."

He fell silent for a moment. "Holler if you need anything," he said heading out.

She watched him through the dust-covered window. How in the world were they going to save this ranch? And what if her decision to stay here would mean the bearded man would find her?

Courage, Mara. This is for the best.
Wasn't it?

Levi was surprised to find Jude still on the property. He was leaning on the bumper of his car, boots crossed at the ankle. Levi recognized the look. He had something to say.

"It's just you and me. Do you really think she's safe in Furnace Falls?" Levi asked.

Jude was slow to answer. "Tolerably." When he started to object, Jude raised a palm. "You're not going to persuade her to leave. Everyone she loves is close—brother, parents. She's not the kind of lady to walk away from that for her own self-preservation. Not a coward. And you'll have eyes on her, Levi."

"My eyes didn't keep Seth from getting shot."

A moment of silence crept up between them until Jude spoke. "You told me you thought your accident months ago was meant to kill Mara. Still think so?"

"Yes. I was driving Mara's car, and I'm more and more certain that someone checked out the wreck and left me there, realizing they'd got the wrong driver." He paused and told Jude about the postcard Mara had received about that same time.

A vulture winged across the gold of the late-afternoon sky, and both of them watched it go.

"Keep your rifle handy," Jude said. "Beckett is alerted, and your brother will notice anyone asking around about Mara. Willow, too. Good thing about her staying here is we have allies all over this town."

Levi didn't point out that there hadn't been much help for Beckett when his wife was being terrorized. Then again, until recently, the townsfolk had believed Beckett was a serial killer. "So you aren't convinced the bearded guy has taken off?"

Jude shrugged. "This doesn't smell right. I believe what I said earlier. I think she's safer here with your eyes on her than in a hotel somewhere. Could be I'm on the wrong track entirely, but I feel better knowing you're gonna be watching out for her...if she'll let you," he added with a wry grin.

As Jude drove away, Levi went to load his

rifle. He didn't need to ask Mara's permission. He was going to look out for her whether or not she wanted him to.

"I promise, Seth. She'll be safe."

FIVE

Mara put the bag on the wooden chest of drawers. She had to force the top one open to install her meager belongings so she left it a tiny bit ajar in case it got stuck again. Not much to unpack. All she had was a change of clothes and toiletries for one night. The memory of that bullet fracturing the window, of Seth's soft cry, made her dizzy. An overwhelming sense of panic began to ripple up her spine. She sat on the cot to catch her breath. Her wrist and shoulders ached, and she longed for a leisurely soak. There was no tub in the bathroom, only a cramped shower behind a new curtain printed with audacious orange poppies.

She smiled. One of the quick additions Levi had asked Willow to provide, probably. Had she been too pushy demanding to stay here? Was it even wise to be living alone on the ranch with only Levi for company in the ramshackle main house? But it was the only thing she could do for her brother, her only living sibling and best friend.

She squirmed into the wee shower and let the tepid water rinse her troubled thoughts away. Putting on clean clothes lifted her spirits. She pulled her wet hair off her face with a hairband and grabbed her phone. There were no new updates on Seth.

Lord, please... Tears choked off the rest of the prayer.

It was barely six, and she longed to take a walk, to explore this run-down property that Seth had sunk every last penny into. It wouldn't be smart to do any solo walking. She opened her laptop, which had fortunately survived the crash, to read up on the details of Camp Town Days. It was indeed the largest organized event in Death Valley. The hotels would be full, and guests would enjoy a number of amenities from tours of the Salt Flats and the Borax mine to moonlight chuck-wagon feasts and even jeep tours. Somehow during her time in Furnace Falls, she had never experienced Camp Town Days, thanks to her father's aversion to crowds and the fact that they traveled every November to visit their grandparents for Thanksgiving. She was impressed by the level of planning and forethought that had obviously gone into the event. Still, she thought with a sigh, one megafestival wasn't going to be enough to drag the ranch into profitability. She wasn't sure anything would be enough, but she was determined that when Seth woke up, the ranch's situation would have at least improved.

Nails scrabbled at the door, and she jumped. A peek out the window revealed Banjo scraping at the wood while Levi tried to stop him.

She opened it.

His cheeks flushed through his tan. "Sorry. Dog hasn't got any manners."

"That's okay. You know I like animals." She dropped to her knees and scratched him under his boney chin. Levi told her about how he'd come to be Banjo's owner.

"Named him after a dog we had when I was a kid."

The conversation dried up at that point. When the silence became awkward, he said "Seth told me you studied to be a vet tech before you worked at your parents' store."

She sighed and got to her feet. "I'd just gotten started when Corinne left. My mom was devastated, and things began to slide at the furniture store, so I quit vet-tech school and went to work there instead."

"Miss the animals?"

"Desperately, but I was needed elsewhere." She shrugged. "End of story."

"Oh. Well, we got plenty of animals here, horses aside." He paused. "I, um, figured you hadn't had dinner, and I'm cooking pasta. Would you like to join me?" He shifted. "Or I can bring you a plate here, you know, if you'd rather."

Eating a meal with Levi was not on the top of her list, but it was a kind offer, and they had to find some common ground. "Tell you what. Will you throw in a quick tour of the ranch before dinner?"

He appeared surprised. "I'd be happy to, but let's wait until morning."

"Why?"

He shrugged. "Better visibility. Less shadows."

Less danger. She suppressed a shiver remembering the bearded man's question. *Why aren't you dead?*

"We can see it on horseback if you still ride," Levi added.

"Yes, I still ride."

He led her across the small dirt area to the main house. So close, she thought. She'd been hoping the cabin was tucked in some remote ranch corner, but it was a stone's throw. The main house was worn, newly repaired shingles standing out against the old ones. Inside was cramped but clean, a small kitchen table, two chairs and a sofa; a bit of the hallway could be seen, which she assumed led to a bedroom and bath. Her eyes were immediately drawn to a wall which was hung with long floor-to-ceiling tubes that sprouted lush bunches of lettuces and herbs. On the floor was an oblong tank filled with glimmering fish and aquatic plants, and rubber tubes maintained some sort of filtration system.

"What is going on here?" she asked, fingering the tender leaves.

"It's aquaponics. I try to be as self-sufficient as possible, and the climate's just too harsh to support crops without a ton of effort. I have enough work to do, so I set up this system. Fish provide fertilizer, and the water gets pumped up the tubes. We have plenty of sunshine here," he said with a grin. "That's one thing Furnace Falls has in abundance. Sun plus water and fertilizer and bingo, greens whenever I want them."

He'd made an oasis in the desert. "You always were a dreamer, Levi." He gave her a sharp look and she realized that perhaps she'd made it sound derogatory. And it was, wasn't it? Levi and her brother had put everything into the Rocking Horse dream, when her brother knew next to nothing about ranching or horses. Same friend who had convinced her brother in high school that they should enter a chili cook-off when neither one of them had ever cooked the stuff before.

He kept his eyes on the pot he was filling with water. "Sometimes dreams come true, if God wants them to. That's why I got this place. My uncle had to sell it while I was still in the service, but then I got my chance when the second owner left."

She tried to put the question politely. "Your siblings didn't want to go in on it with you?"

"No. They aren't as into horses as I am."

Or perhaps they had enough sense to recognize a losing proposition when they saw one. "And you really feel like you can make it profitable?"

"Right now I am aiming for self-sufficient. It's a ranch, Mara. It's never going to be a lucrative business. That's not the point."

It is if you convince your best friend to bankrupt himself to save it, she thought with a flash of annoyance, but she didn't want to get into a discussion on the merits of the Rocking Horse. When she offered to help, he directed her to pick some basil and greens. The tender leaves snapped off easily until she had a bowlful.

"Pick some kale, also. Too bitter for me, but we're gonna have a visitor who likes it."

"A visitor?"

He left the pot to boil and stepped out on the

porch with her. He placed a pile of kale on the weathered wood and drew her back with a finger to his lips. There was a scraping noise, and a small rabbit, head crowned with two enormous ears, appeared over the top of the porch. In a flash, the animal had snatched the greens and returned to his hidey-hole under the porch.

Banjo raced to the edge of the porch barking into the hole until he tired of the game.

"Fortunately, Banjo is slower than Rabbit," Levi said. "I haven't been able to convince the dog that he's his brother from another mother."

She had to giggle at that one. "Did you adopt Rabbit, too?"

"Nah. He showed up here one day. He's got part of a front paw missing, so he needs the shelter of my porch, I think. Wouldn't make it too long in Death Valley. Figured I had greens to spare."

"He needs a better name than Rabbit."

"Maybe you can think of one. I'm just the food provider."

Levi poured kibble into a bowl for Banjo and joined her at the table with two plates of butter-and-basil sprinkled spaghetti along with a green salad. Her head still pounded, and her stomach roiled from the ongoing tension of worrying about Seth, but she ate a portion of the meal and found it delicious.

Here in this worn country kitchen with a dog lazing in a corner of waning sunlight and the comfortable conversation with Levi, her troubles seemed far away.

They're not, Mara. Your brother is fighting for his life, and the shooter is out there somewhere, waiting for a chance to take another crack at you. This isn't safe. This isn't home.

"Let me help with the dishes," she said and ignored his protest.

Dishes done, he walked her back to her tiny shack where he insisted on adjusting the air-conditioning which didn't seem to be performing to standard. He handled the job quickly. "Easier than working on an army vehicle," he said.

She flashed back to the moment when Seth announced that he was enlisting with Levi. Her sister Corinne had been sixteen at the time and was already showing a stubborn streak a mile wide. She remembered her own angry tears, as a newly minted eighteen-year-old. "You are not going away, Seth. You just can't." But he could and he did, and sullen Corinne had acted out even more. Once she had even disappeared for an entire weekend, and no amount of chastising or grounding had caused her to reveal where she'd been.

Mara realized Levi was speaking. "You look… angry."

"Not angry. Just thinking back on how my family's lives changed when Seth joined the army. Corinne acted out, became desperate almost, for attention."

Levi looked at the floor. "That must have been hard."

"Yes," she said stiffly. "It was. After what happened, I think my parents wondered if things would have been different with Corinne if Seth had been around. I was furious at you for talking him into enlisting."

Levi cocked his head. "Other way around."

"What?"

"He enlisted first and convinced me to join him."

She gaped. How had she gotten that backward? "I didn't know that." Looking into the blue of his eyes, her pulse fluttered. She suddenly wondered what else she'd gotten wrong about Levi Duke.

But it didn't matter about the past. All that was left was the present. She shook off the feelings and put on a businesslike tone. "Meeting in town tomorrow at ten? Ranch tour before then?"

He nodded. "Maybe pull the curtains and turn the bolt. Precautions, is all." He opened the door and whistled. Banjo came barreling into the small room, skidding to a stop at her feet. "Since you and 'Jo have hit it off, figured he could be your roomie. Don't let him on the bed, though. Give him an inch, and he'll take a mile."

She was going to protest, but deep down she did not want to be left alone in the silent cabin. "All right, Banjo. But you heard what Levi said about the sleeping arrangements."

She waited for Levi to leave and did as he asked. As she looked out the window at the darkening landscape, she saw movement as Rabbit ventured out to sniff at the grass. She felt a kinship to the vulnerable creature. Who knew what was lurking in the shadows, looking for prey?

With a shiver, she yanked the drapes closed.

Levi was up before the sun. He'd already saddled the horses, Sunny and Pumpkin Pie, his two sweetest mounts. He'd left out a carrot for Rabbit, and the creature emerged from his hidey-hole to snatch up the treat before Banjo bounded out from Mara's cabin, Mara right behind him. Good timing. Levi set out the dog's morning kibble, and once again Banjo wolfed it down in moments.

Mara walked toward him. She looked more rested but groggy. She still moved tentatively, as if she was sore.

"Is there any update on Seth?"

"Mom said she thinks he's breathing a little better."

Better. Good. He'd take any bit of hope God would give them. "Would you like some breakfast?"

She shook her head and yawned. "I'm fine, thank you. Ready for that ride around the ranch."

"Maybe..." he started. "I mean since you just got out of the hospital..."

She shot him *that look*, and he stopped talking and offered her his cupped hands for her to climb into the saddle. She surprised him by accepting. He lifted gently, marveling at how slight and athletic she was. The saddle suited her, he thought, then shook the admiration aside.

Banjo trotted along next to him as they skirted the corral and then headed out to the pasture. He wished the fence posts did not look quite so worn and the secondhand watering trough he'd acquired wasn't dented on one side. At least the horses were their usual patient, well-behaved selves. "We're in prime visitor season, of course. People want tours of the park and surroundings."

"How many people?"

He hesitated.

"Data, Levi. How many tours have you booked this season so far?"

"Ten." He felt, rather than saw, her dismay as he kept his gaze fixed on the horizon.

"Ten? How can you even pay for horse feed?"

As a matter of fact, he couldn't. He'd dipped

into his savings and taken a second job for a while at the local garage to swing it. "I'm not the only stable in the area. Besides, it will get better. My cousin had some trouble at the Hotsprings, and people weren't staying, but that's all past. Camp Town Days are coming. Business is picking up. After today's meeting, the bookings will start coming in through our web page."

"I went over the website and all the files last night, after you gave me the passwords. Who designed the website?"

He felt his cheeks warm. "I did. Bought a book called *Websites for Dummies* so it was written just for me. It was like trying to push a boulder uphill, but I finally got it done."

Her good-natured laughter seemed to mingle with the cool of the morning. Encouraged, he put his best spin on the tour, highlighting the new saddles and the qualities of the other nine horses that were munching on the hay he'd scattered that morning. She didn't say much, but she pitched in to unsaddle and groom their horses when they returned, before they loaded up in his truck.

"No, 'Jo," he called to the dog. "You stay here and keep watch, huh?"

Banjo tipped his wedge of a head as if to say, "You have to ask?"

They drove slowly off the ranch and onto the

main road. As they passed the Hotsprings Hotel, he noticed several cars in the parking lot. Finally, Beckett and Laney seemed to be gaining ground, as he'd told Mara. They'd earned it. Never had he seen two people so deeply in love, except maybe his parents. After forty years, his father still lit up whenever his mom returned from a trip or errand.

"I got my honeybunch home," he would say.

The sentiment always awakened a kind of longing in Levi. He'd never been much for dating. Girls made him so nervous, he rarely gathered up the courage to ask one out. Mara was different, though. His other attractions came and went, but he'd never quite been able to forget the dark-haired girl who was his best friend's sister. Seth hadn't said much when Levi asked Mara to the senior prom. He wondered all of a sudden what he would say if they'd started a relationship. Thinking about Mara made Levi's mind wander into confusing circles. He regripped the wheel and focused hard on the road. It wasn't the time to be distracted, that was for certain.

He'd remembered to stow his rifle in the back of the truck, covered by an old barn blanket. But nothing would happen today, he reassured himself. They'd be in town with plenty of people around.

Including the one who had shot Seth and tried to kill Mara?

His teeth ground together.

I've got her back, Seth. Don't you worry.

SIX

Furnace Falls was not much changed, Mara noted. The small town tucked at the edge of the Nevada side of the Death Valley National Park provided the basic necessities minus many frills. There was a post office, a health clinic, a gas station and a couple of eateries surrounded by a whole lot of sunbaked acreage and the spectacular Funeral Mountain Range. The pastel-painted Sweet Shop was new since they'd moved away, and a veterinary hospital now stood on the corner that had been an empty lot when Mara was in high school. The miniscule A's Art Studio caught her attention, the planters outside the door bursting with wildly twisted cactus.

Levi parked the truck outside the Grange Hall, next to a dozen other cars. The yellow stonework of the building glowed in the morning sunlight. A cluster of pines rustled in the breeze as they crossed the sun-splashed patio. Inside, the rows of folding chairs were nearly full of people, including plenty of bearded men. Fear hit her like a blow. She gasped and drew back. Her mind might have forgotten, but her body had not… She'd almost been murdered by a man like this.

Her brain replayed the hateful words. *Why aren't you dead?*

Levi held her arm. "All the participants from the Mule Team reenactment try to look the part. I should have thought to warn you."

She forced her breathing to steady. There were probably fifteen men, faces hidden by bushy facial hair and floppy felt hats. Memories of the wreck, of the hands that covered her mouth in the hospital erupted, leaving her suddenly cold.

"Do you recognize anyone?"

"More like everyone," she said. But the man wouldn't be here, would he? Even if he was, she'd be safe with plenty of witnesses around. She felt more at ease with Levi holding her arm. He wasn't forcing her in, merely standing, allowing her to proceed or to retreat. Jude waved from a corner of the room. She exhaled. Nothing would happen, and none of these men wanted her dead.

Did they?

Yet another man with a beard and hat climbed to the podium. "For any of you who don't know me, I'm Gene Warrington, and I have the honor of chairing this amazing event this year." There were whoops and claps from the audience. "I'm a newbie in this role, so I hope you'll be patient with my mistakes. Honored that you're all here and taking part. Let's dive into the schedule first. That ought to take an hour or so to debrief. Lunch will be provided, thanks to the Hotsprings Hotel, and the afternoon will wrap up with a ride along the route to check the terrain. We had some ground failure so keep a look out for it. Plenty of time for you all to retrieve your horses and trailer them over." He gestured to a helper to start up a PowerPoint, which was projected onto the wall. Mara made notes, mentally configuring how to maximize the involvement for the Rocking Horse. She became so wrapped up in the details she almost missed the slender man who raised his hand. He was clean-shaven, hair long enough to touch his shoulders.

"Not to interrupt, Dad, but I just wanted to introduce myself. I'm Teegan Warrington, and I'm organizing the vendor fair, which will be staged inside the Grange Hall. See me during the lunch break for details."

Mara did not realize she'd dropped the notepad on which she'd been furiously scribbling.

Shock hit her like a hammer blow.

Levi leaned close and whispered in her ear. "What's wrong?"

She couldn't answer. Fortunately, the room

was still darkened to accommodate the PowerPoint. The need to escape overwhelmed her, and she hurried out of the hall, Levi following.

She made it to the shade of the pines and tried to talk sense to herself. It couldn't be, but it was. What did it mean?

Levi bent and gently lifted her chin. "Mara, tell me what's wrong."

"I'm not sure. This can't be right."

"What?"

"Teegan Warrington."

"The guy who's running the vendor fair?"

She nodded, her heartbeat still thundering in her chest. "He was my sister Corinne's crush back in high school before she…"

Levi finished her thought. "Before she disappeared."

"Yes." The word came out as a whisper around the clog in her throat.

Jude joined them. "Everything okay?"

Levi filled him in.

Jude settled his sheriff's cap more firmly on his head. "That must feel strange, but it's not a complete surprise. Plenty of people stick close to their hometowns. Your folks moved to Henderson at the end of Corrine's sophomore year, right? That's where you lived when she ran off?"

Mara nodded. "Yes. Our last day here was a

couple of weeks after my high-school graduation."

"I didn't work for Inyo County back then, but I did some looking into the file after your accident. If I recall correctly, the cops interviewed Teegan, and he had an alibi. He said he hadn't seen Corrine at all before she disappeared, and there was no one to disprove that."

Mara had read the police file, too. She imagined a million different scenarios of what might have happened. Now another scenario flicked to life. Corinne tracked Teegan down; he rejected her. Despondent, she drove into Death Valley and wandered off into a desolate canyon to die or found one of the thousands of small trails and never made it back.

Guilt wormed up from the dreary place where she kept it locked up. They used to be so close, she and Corinne. They shared clothes, pooled their allowances to buy a flimsy backyard pool, split countless peanut butter and banana sandwiches as midnight snacks. How had they become so estranged that her baby sister had not confided her level of hopelessness? Not disclosed that she was in love?

Mara had known Corinne was upset about something in the weeks before she left home. It wasn't unusual. She'd been difficult since they'd moved to Henderson, just before Seth deployed.

Sixteen-year-old Corinne had been moody, sullen, defiant. It was natural, she'd told herself, for a young teen uprooted from her high-school friends. Corinne had written dozens of letters, secretly mailing them without letting Mara see the address. Could she have been writing to Teegan? As far as Mara knew, the two had attended some games and rallies their first few years in high school, but her parents discouraged them from doing any dating since Corinne was so young.

Some of Mara's unease began to ebb. "You're right. It makes sense that I would run into him, I guess. I didn't know he'd stayed here in Furnace Falls, but like you said, that isn't uncommon. It's his hometown."

Levi frowned. "I don't know the family well. They moved here when Teegan was in sixth grade or so, as I recall. Gene is in the long-haul trucking business, owns a company. He lives well outside of town. My mother knew his wife, I think. She died of cancer just after Teegan started high school."

So Teegan's mom had been dying of cancer when Corinne met him. That could certainly explain why he hadn't been as eager to keep a long-distance connection with Corinne as she'd been with him. He'd had a lot going on.

Levi looked closely at her. "If it's too much right now, Mara, I can take you home."

It *was* too much, worrying about her brother and having all the memories of Corinne circling like restless birds, but she wasn't about to fold up and let the past divert her from helping Seth now. She shook her head. "I'm fine. Let's go back to the meeting. I want to hear about the high-traffic events where we can put out flyers."

Jude grinned. "A mind for business. That's what your dusty old ranch needs, Levi."

Levi shot him a look. "Thanks."

"Just call 'em like I see 'em." Jude put a finger to his cap and headed for his car. "I'll check on you later."

The next couple of hours passed swiftly enough, but Mara was continually distracted by Teegan. When they broke for lunch, everyone piled out of the auditorium to find long tables set out and Beckett Duke and his helper Herm manning a massive barbecue. The smell of burgers reminded her she'd skipped breakfast. A woman with long honey-colored hair twisted into a soft braid approached. Her rounded belly and the kiss she'd dropped on Beckett's cheek indicated she must be Laney Duke, Beckett's wife.

She clasped her hands together. "Mara, I am just so sorry about the accident. I've been praying for you and Seth."

Mara couldn't help but smile at Laney's infectious warmth. "Thank you. He's holding his own, and I'm almost back to normal."

She beamed at Levi. "Well, you've got a great partner in Levi. He cares for everything and everyone."

She wanted to break in and discourage the notion that she and Levi were partners, but Laney was bubbling on.

"Please come to the Hotsprings sometime. We'd love to have you, and if there's anything we can do…" She was interrupted when a little boy bumped into her leg.

"Oopsy," Laney said. "I don't see everything below my belly button anymore. What's up, Peter?"

The dark-haired child was probably no more than five. His front tooth looked a bit snaggly, as if it was loose. "Ketchup pwease, ma'am."

Mara smiled at his adorable lisp as a woman appeared, a sun hat shading her fair skin. "Did he say *please*? We're working on manners."

"Yes, Amelia, he sure did." Laney handed over a bottle of ketchup to the boy. "I think you know Levi, but this is his friend Mara."

Was it her imagination, or did Laney imbue the word *friend* with a special something? It surprised her to think of Levi as a friend when she was supposed to be angry at him for manipulating her brother. She was still mad at him…wasn't she? Was Laney trying to be some sort of matchmaker? But her smile was wide and innocent.

Mara shook hands with Amelia. The woman was tall and thin, nose sprinkled with freckles. A long column of hair was collected by a flowered scarf that trailed down her back.

"I'm pleased to meet you," Amelia said. "There are so many new people this year. It's our first time as a Camp Town vendor. It was too much before with Peter being so young. I'm an artist. We're selling my watercolors."

"So you know Teegan, the man who's organizing the vendors?" The question tumbled out before Mara had a chance to think it over. Her interest in Teegan would not abate for some reason.

Amelia laughed. "I know him well," she said. "He's my husband, and this is our son."

Mara tried to smile back. She was trying to think of what exactly to say next, when Teegan approached, a burger held in one hand. He scrubbed a hand over his razor-burned chin, rubbing at a drop of ketchup below his lip. As he got a look at her, his face paled, and he twitched as if he'd been given an electric shock. His mouth opened in a little *o* of surprise.

No need for more introductions. It seemed that Teegan Warrington knew exactly who she was.

* * *

Levi was close enough that he could feel the tension radiating off Mara. He offered his hand to Teegan to give Mara some time to recover. "Levi Duke. We're running the horses for Camp Town this year. And this is—"

"Mara Castillo," Teegan finished.

Amelia's eyes went wide. "Corinne Castillo's sister?"

"Yes," Mara said. "Did you know her?"

"No. I mean, well, we never met. I moved here at the end of my senior year, but I remember hearing that she disappeared."

Teegan looked pained. "I didn't realize you'd come back to town."

Mara explained about helping the Rocking Horse. That seemed to set Teegan more at ease.

"Oh. Just here for a while, then. Hope you enjoy it." He frowned. "We heard about your accident. Real sorry about that."

Amelia nodded. "How is your brother? That was a terrible thing."

"Holding his own," Mara said.

"Glad to hear it." Teegan patted his wife's arm. "Honey, Peter should eat his lunch. We'll be busy after the break."

"Sure," Amelia said, casting one more unsettled look on Mara. "Come on, Peter. Let's go sit and eat our lunch. Daddy will join us later."

She hefted her son, ketchup bottle and all, onto her hip. As she whirled away, she bumped into Gene Warrington who clutched a hot dog in one hand. He winced and steadied her as she righted herself.

"Sorry, Grandpa."

"That's okay," he said, winking at Peter. "Save me a hot dog, will you?" He walked over. "Everyone doing okay over here?"

"Sure, Dad," Teegan said hastily. "This is Levi Duke and Mara Castillo. I, uh, went to high school with her sister for a while."

Gene raised an eyebrow and offered a wry grin. "Nice. How are you and your sister?"

"My sister's dead," Mara said flatly.

Gene blanched. "Oh, I am sorry. Folks around here will tell you I am famous for inserting my booted foot squarely in my mouth."

Mara sighed. "It's okay. You didn't know."

His mouth quirked in thought. "Wait, I remember that name now. Corinne Castillo, right? The police came to ask questions, and we sure kept our eyes out for that young lady, but we never did find her. I didn't put it together that she was your sister. Please accept my apologies. Big Mouth Warrington strikes again."

Teegan wiped his brow. "Hey, Dad, I think they're looking for you at the info table."

Gene nodded. "I'd better go. Again, I apologize for my remarks. It's good to have you here, and I hope Camp Town Days will be a great experience for you."

Levi edged closer to Mara, wondering if it was all getting to be too much for her to handle, so soon out of the hospital. He needn't have worried.

"When was the last time you saw my sister, Teegan?" she asked.

Teegan's Adam's apple bobbed. "A few times the end of our sophomore year, just before you left town. I told the police that when they came around. Why do you ask?"

Mara shrugged. "I wanted to put together her last few days in my mind. For some reason, I thought she might have headed to Furnace Falls to see you the day she disappeared."

"To see me?" Teegan's lip curled. "I'll tell you nicely because you're her sister and I know you must be grieved by what happened. I never saw her again after she left for Henderson. That's what I told the cops, and that's the truth." He leaned closer. "I have a family and a business here, so don't come around making trouble."

Levi was nose to nose with him in an instant. "Step back." He did not raise his voice in the slightest, but Teegan must have been able to sense his intensity. "You're out of line, and I don't like your tone." He said the last bit so low he figured it would stay between the two of them.

Teegan eased away, a tentative smile forming. "I don't want any trouble."

Levi did not move. "Then, we want the same thing. No trouble, just answers."

"I don't have any. I dated her a few times when I was a teen. She's dead. That's all I know."

Mara said "Can we talk more? Meet privately?"

Teegan kept moving away. "I am very busy. I have to go now."

He walked hurriedly into the Grange Hall, not stopping to look back.

Mara blew out a breath. "What did you make of that?"

"I think he doesn't want to talk to you."

"Why would that be?"

Because he knows something he's not telling. Aloud Levi said "Not sure. Let's eat something and go get the horses."

He led Mara to a table and fetched them both a couple of the sloppy hamburgers Beckett was busily grilling.

She toyed with her napkin and stared at the burger and the bowl of beans.

"Don't like it?" he inquired.

"It's not the food." She hesitated. "I appreciate you standing up to Teegan for me, Levi. That was kind of you. But I don't want you to feel like you have to do that. I can speak for myself."

"I know. Just isn't acceptable for a man to speak in that tone to any woman."

Her cheeks went pink. He liked the color, soft like the little wildflowers that popped up in the spring. He realized he was staring at her so he drank some lemonade.

"So you stand up for all women, do you?"

He had to look again at the flush in her cheeks, her eyes the color of the perfect cup of black coffee. "Yes, ma'am, but you're Seth's sister, so that's another reason." He tried to think for a moment what he'd said that made her look away. The delicate way her brows drew together and the troubled frown made him wish he could have encouraged a smile instead. Then he'd be able to see that light spark and hear her laugh again.

His own thoughts startled him. He was supposed to be impressing her with his ranching acumen and keeping her safe until Seth made it through. That was all. Refocusing, he sipped his lemonade hoping the cold drink would clear his mental muddle. It went down the wrong pipe, and he coughed violently.

Smooth, Levi.

His coughing having subsided, they started in on their lunch. He was a couple of bites into his burger when he felt the hairs prickle on the back of his neck. He craned around and saw Teegan staring at Mara with an expression he could not fully decipher.

Uncertainty?

Fear?

Whatever it was, Levi intended to keep Teegan in his sights.

Friends close, and enemies closer…

SEVEN

Mara would not admit to Levi that her head was throbbing as they unloaded the horses from the trailer in an empty field near the Borax mine that afternoon. The ride would be a quick overview of part of the trail. Fortunately, the reenactment was only an approximation of the real thing. In actuality, the historical 20 Mule Teams made a grueling ten-day trip, hauling tons of the mineral from the Harmony Borax Works just outside of town to the railhead some hundred and sixty-five miles away.

Today they would be riding from the Borax Works to the main visitor campsite and back. She was grateful it would only be a couple of hours' adventure, since her body was still complaining from the wreck. Stabs of fear cut at her at unexpected moments. Her brother, her best friend. Would he ever wake up?

She'd called the hospital again and promised to visit the next day, blinking back tears to hear that he was still comatose. She didn't want to cry publicly, and for some reason it was harder to be stoic with Levi solicitously checking on her comfort. When he looked at her with those somber blue eyes, it made something inside her go soft and emotional. It reminded her that in the years following her high-school graduation, she'd been hard-pressed to get the gangly, silent cowboy out of her thoughts. What would have happened between them if she hadn't moved away?

Don't forget what did happen, she told herself with a shake. All this time she'd thought Levi had lured her brother into the service and then roped him into a worthless ranch. Even if she'd been mistaken about who'd talked who into enlisting, the latter was still true, and she was wise not to forget it.

Teegan and his unwelcoming reaction was a distraction. *Get this ranch on its feet, Mara, so Seth will have something to wake up for.*

"I can do this alone," Levi was saying. "We can get you a ride to the hospital if you need to be there."

"I want to see the route," she said.

"Sure, but—"

"Levi," she stopped saddling Pumpkin Pie and looked at him. She meant to give him a firm brush-off, to remind him exactly why she was there, but there was that blue intensity again, and something about his long, lean face and the way he looked at her that made her forget. "Thank you," she said instead. "I know this is not how you meant things to go. I'll try to be pleasant company. No guarantees, but I'll do my best."

He ducked his head, and she thought she caught the corner of a smile. "I'm happy to have you along."

Happy? He didn't exactly meet her eye, but she smiled, anyway. "Brings back memories. Remember when we went fishing instead of senior prom?"

His laugh was deep and sonorous. "Yes, I recall we had to drive three hours in Austin's truck to find a fishing spot and the engine overheated twice."

"I guess a fishing expedition when you live in the desert wasn't the wisest plan."

"Fun, though. Never enjoyed a drive so much in my life."

He'd enjoyed the drive? Now it was her turn to look away as she mounted Pumpkin Pie before he could help her. "We didn't catch a single fish."

He settled into the saddle as if he'd been born there, fluid, graceful, as if horse and rider were one being. "That wasn't the important part." He led his horse toward a group of others astride their animals.

It wasn't? Mara set her wonderment aside

as they joined the throng riding past the Borax mines. She saw Gene calling out directions. Was Teegan out there, too? She moved her horse closer to Levi's. The trail was relatively flat and accessible even for the replica wagons that traveled with them, pulled by sets of sturdy donkeys. She'd forgotten the sheer vastness of Death Valley and its surrounds. Wide-open, so much less populated than Henderson, and with a mysterious quality that made her insides unwind a bit. The strange desert sun that seemed to shine differently—was it the air? She pulled in a deep lungful and murmured a silent prayer that Seth would live to see it again.

The temperature was in the mid-seventies, warm enough to permeate her muscles with a comfortable ease. The sky was cloudless, empty except for the wrens that skimmed the landscape looking for a meal. A jackrabbit poked his head above a hunk of rock and surveyed the intruders, whiskers twitching. She thought about Rabbit and how quickly he would be devoured if Levi hadn't provided a home and shelter.

Two hours passed with companionable chatter. The shock of being surrounded by men who looked like the one who had attacked her began to subside. There were a few women as well, eagerly conversing as they rode along. She caught a glimpse of Teegan. As soon as he connected glances with her, he immediately urged his horse into a faster gait and left her behind. Levi was somehow always close, no matter how many people milled along on the trail.

As they headed into the third hour on the trail, they passed through an open wrought iron gate. The name on the stout mailbox read *Warrington*.

"Welcome to my place," Gene said. "We'll take a pit stop here. There's water for the horses and lemonade and cookies for everyone else. The route crosses over my property another mile and cuts around the canyon to checkpoint two, the starting point for the Mule Team ride into town. There's a nice flat area there for those of you rugged types who are camping out. A few tents are still available for rental, but most are spoken for by out-of-towners. I can promise you lots of fresh air, sunshine and the occasional tarantula." The gathering chuckled. "Oh, and we brought in some porta-potties. I know it's a modern touch, but I don't want anyone getting bitten by a rattlesnake while taking care of business in the wild. I'm hosting a catered dinner on Saturday night right here to thank you all for being a part of this great event. Sound good?"

The enthusiastic whoops rose in a chorus.

"Gonna fix your famous brisket?" a man cried out.

Gene laughed. "Famous or infamous, I'm fixing it. Bring your Tums."

Mara noticed Teegan did not join in the merriment. His attention was focused elsewhere. Ahead was a sprawling one-story Spanish-style home with stuccoed walls and an enclosed patio shaded by shaggy trees. Sharing the same paved circular drive was a smaller house, similar in style. It had its own enclosed porch, and in the front yard there was a long table covered by a cloth, holding pitchers of lemonade and platters of cookies. Amelia stood there wearing a straw hat and waving. Peter rode circles on his tiny bike as he took in the spectacle. The participants had begun to tie their horses to the hitching posts and help themselves to cookies and lemonade.

She dismounted with Levi and walked to the table. Amelia's shocked look when she'd introduced herself made her wonder if Amelia knew more about Corinne than she let on and it was not just her imagination that Teegan was avoiding her. Waiting her turn in line, she'd almost reached the front when Amelia's gaze fastened on her, and the smile faltered.

"Hi. Um, I have to help Peter with something. Please have some cookies."

Abruptly she left her post and called to Peter. He came, and she led him by the hand into the house, shutting the door behind them.

Levi raised an eyebrow at Mara. "Not very hospitable."

"Maybe it's just the fact that I represent Teegan's ex-girlfriend. But her reaction seems sort of extreme."

They helped themselves to lemonade and a cookie while they looked at the dirt trail cut into the dry earth across Gene's property. "Big place," Levi said. "Gene said it's close to three hundred acres."

"Big enough for Teegan to live on the same property as his father," she mused. "I wonder why they don't share the main house."

"They don't get on sometimes," a voice put in.

A heavyset man with a scruff of well-tended beard downed a cup of lemonade. He wore a long-sleeved flannel shirt, and perspiration shone on his face. "Name's Jerry. We talked on the phone."

Mara frowned. "We did?"

"I own J and K Excavation. You called last week to find out who might have sent you that text on my cell phone. The one that said *Marbles*?"

Mara gaped. "Yes. Yes, I did."

He shrugged and rolled a shoulder thoughtfully. "I'm sorry I couldn't help. I still have no idea who coulda done it."

Mara sighed. "It's okay. I appreciate you trying."

Jerry bit into one cookie of the stack he'd taken, his expression thoughtful. "Tell you what, though. I've been mulling over it since I talked to you. There is maybe one more thing I could check."

Mara's nerves prickled. "Really?"

He finished a cookie and wiped his hands on his jeans. "I'm not a very good recordkeeper. I'm a real dinosaur, so my appointments are all scrawled down in ugly old appointment books, rather than on a computer. Old-school, like I said. My shelving unit collapsed last week and sent boxes falling everywhere. I haven't had the time to sort through it all. My appointment book is somewhere in the mess. If you come by sometime, you're welcome to dig through the piles and find it. It would show where I was the day you got that text. Never did find my cell phone. Had to buy a new one."

Mara's pulse quickened. She purposely did not look at Levi. This matter didn't concern him, and she did not want to catch a frown of disapproval on his face. "That would be fabulous. Can I come tomorrow, maybe? It would have to be after I get back from Las Vegas."

He finished his drink and turned to head for the table to get a refill. "Sure. I'll be in the office all afternoon after church, trying to dig myself out."

The participants continued to mill around, but Mara hardly noticed. She whispered to Levi. "I know there's probably nothing in it, but I might as well take him up on his offer."

"As long as I go with you."

She cocked her chin. "Fair enough. I promised I wouldn't go wandering off on my own."

"Yes, you did, and I'm holding you to it."

Her thoughts whirled until it was time to climb into the saddle again. What was it about this town that made her obsess about her sister? Corinne was dead. She had no false hopes that there was any other possibility. If she was still alive, she would have contacted them in the long years since her disappearance. Corinne was young and selfish, impetuous, but she loved their parents, and she would not have tortured them by allowing them to believe her dead. There was nothing at J and K Excavations that would change those facts, but she could not ignore the strong compulsion that was spurring her to check into it, anyway.

She swung a leg over the saddle. Instantly she knew something was wrong. A shock went through the horse. In a flash, animal's ears went back, and she leaped sideways so suddenly that Mara had to cling to the saddle horn to avoid being bucked off. "Whoa, Pumpkin—" she started, but before the words were fully out, the horse began to gallop down the road, leaving the startled participants behind. The ground moved past in a blur. Her instinct was to haul back on the reins, but she knew from experience that would only panic the horse even more.

Instead she sat back deeply in the saddle and tried to hold on. Inexplicably the horse seemed to grow even more frantic, galloping faster until the ground flew by in a dizzying blur.

Stay in the saddle. She focused on that one task, calling out to the horse as loudly as she dared. Thrown toward her left side, she again tried to center herself in the saddle. When she did so, the horse squealed. In pain? She immediately weighted back on her left side. The animal swerved to avoid a branch on the ground and Mara was flopped back toward her right hip. The horse again whinnied as if in pain and ran harder. Using all her strength, Mara leaned to her left side again. The mare continued to speed on, but the squeal of pain ebbed away.

Whatever it took, she had to keep her weight off her right side, while clinging to the horse with all her might.

If she didn't, she might just join her brother in the hospital again.

Hold on, Mara.

* * *

Levi urged his horse into a gallop, praying Mara would be able to hold on. He edged as close as he dared and skimmed out a hand to grab one of the reins. Mara's fingers were white as she gripped the saddle, jaw clenched in concentration. He could see that she would not be able to keep her seat much longer. Stretching as far as he dared, he was able to snag one of the reins.

At first he did not apply pressure, since a yank would startle the horse further, but gradually with the single rein he tugged until the horse veered ever so slightly. Pumpkin's ears were pinned back, her eyes rolling in fear.

"Whoa, Pumpkin," he called gently, continuing to encourage the horse to move in a circle. "I'm gonna help you. Easy, girl. Easy." At first the mare would be led a few steps and then jag out sideways as if she would bolt again, but slowly, gradually, he persuaded the horse to circle and slow. Another half circle and he leaped from Sunny's saddle and jogged next to Pumpkin. "Easy," he crooned, "easy, sweetheart."

He finally coaxed her to an unsteady halt. The horse stood trembling, sweating, appearing as upset as Mara looked as she slid from the saddle.

He squeezed her forearm. "You okay?"

She panted. "Yes."

He tried to both comfort the horse and hang

on to Mara. "I've never seen Pumpkin Pie behave like that."

"Something hurt her, right side," Mara managed. "Check." Reluctantly, he let Mara go. She followed him around, giving the horse a wide berth. Levi's muscles went rigid as he saw the trail of blood trickling from under the saddle.

"Hey, sweetheart," he whispered. "Something hurt you, darling?" He stroked Pumpkin and eased his hand under. She tensed again, but she allowed him to remove the object that had been stuck underneath the saddle blanket.

He held up a pointed metal object, wet with the mare's blood. Anger began to boil up inside him. "It's a jack."

He watched the understanding dawn on her.

"I used to play jacks with Corinne. I didn't think kids played that anymore."

The fury he felt made his head swim. Someone had put the sharp metal piece under Pumpkin's saddle, hoping she would spook. His horse had been hurt, and Mara had barely escaped serious injury. If she'd been less of a horsewoman, she'd have been thrown for sure. Fury pounded through his veins.

Gene, Jerry, Teegan and others caught up to them.

"Some horse you got there," Teegan said. "I wouldn't rent that one out for tours, if I was you."

Levi glowered and held up the jack. "It's not the horse. Someone stuck this under her saddle."

Gene's eyes went wide. "Who would do that?"

"Everyone here is a horse lover," Jerry added.

Others moved closer. One man pulled off his hat and scratched his head. "I got a kit. Want me to take a look at the wound?"

"No one touches this horse," Levi said. He looked at Mara. "She could have been killed."

Gene huffed. "But…it must have been some sort of accident. There's no way—"

"No accident. Someone put it there." Levi's eyes met Teegan's. "Does your son have a game of jacks that's missing a piece?"

Teegan went rigid. "I don't like what you're insinuating."

"And I don't like what just happened to Mara and my horse."

Gene stepped between them. "Easy, gentlemen. Levi, I am positive no one here caused this accident. Probably the jack got stuck to your saddle blanket somehow after that last camp you ran for the kids, and you didn't notice it." Gene looked relieved as if he'd found a solution. "I'll call the police right now, if you want to be extra cautious."

"I'm taking my horse back to the ranch to treat her. I'll call Jude from there." The anger still roared in his senses.

"Yeah. Tell him your theory about someone sticking a jack under the saddle. That will really entertain him." Teegan's smile was mirthless.

Levi felt like knocking the smug smile right off Teegan's face. He didn't realize he'd taken a step toward him until Mara circled his wrist with her fingers. "Let's go, Levi. Pumpkin needs attention, and I'm okay. Come on."

He allowed himself to be persuaded. They walked the horses back to the house, and Levi called Austin to drive the horse trailer from the Borax mine to meet them. While they waited, Levi made sure Mara sat in the shade with a bottle of water, while he urged Pumpkin Pie and Sonny to drink from the trough.

He saw the curtains of the small house flick slightly. Was Amelia watching them? Had it been her that stuck the jack under the saddle while people were busy drinking lemonade and eating cookies? Or Teegan? Or someone else he hadn't identified yet as an enemy?

A warm breeze enveloped him, bringing the scent of long-dried earth. Death Valley had always been a place of security, acceptance, peace. Now he felt a tinge of something in the air he'd never felt before in his small town.

Danger.

EIGHT

Austin and Levi talked quietly when he arrived to the front area of Gene's property and trailered the horses. It was the first time she'd seen the genial smile gone from Austin's handsome face. He opened the passenger door of Levi's truck for her.

"I've never known Levi to be that angry in my whole life," Austin said quietly while Levi locked the horse trailer doors. "Glad you're okay, Mara."

Mara gave him a nod and smile and climbed in the truck.

Levi slowly drove away. She could see the vein in his temple throbbing and rage in his knitted ginger brows.

"The horse will be okay. I'll help you tend her wound," she started.

"Doesn't matter," he snapped. "Someone hurt my horse and might have killed you." He reached out and gripped her fingers. His hand was warm and calloused, swallowing hers inside his big palm. His grasp was almost painful until he seemed to realize it and relaxed his hold. He pulled her fingers to his mouth and brushed a kiss on her knuckle. She felt a rush of surprise. A long moment of silence played between them.

"And I didn't even wander off on my own, did I?" Her attempt to lighten the mood did not work at first, until a tiny smile tugged at his mouth and he released her hand.

"No, you were right next to me. I must be some kind of idiot not to have seen someone messing with Pumpkin's saddle."

"No fault of yours. I didn't see it, either. Anyone could have done it. Why, though? To scare me out of participating in Camp Town Days? Or to frighten me out of town?"

They did not come to any conclusions as they returned to the Rocking Horse. She accepted an enthusiastic and slobbery welcome from Banjo as Levi unloaded the horses. The dog followed her to the pasture. Inside the barn, she took Pumpkin's reins. "Let me treat her wound, while you give Sunny a rubdown."

Levi hesitated.

"I'm good with horses, remember?"

With a nod, he handed her a box with first-aid supplies. She unsaddled the horse and took a moment to stroke a soft brush over the animal's sides, staying away from the wound. Levi filled two buckets with oats for each horse. Pumpkin munched contentedly while she inspected the puncture. "Not deep. We just need to clean it out and watch for any signs of infection." Filling a bottle with cold water, she cleansed the wound and applied a diluted Betadine solution before she covered it with a gauze bandage. "I'll check it daily, but I think she'll heal up on her own." With gentle fingers she caressed the horse's neck. "I'm sorry, Pumpkin. You didn't deserve to be hurt today." She found Levi staring at her.

"You haven't lost your touch," he said. "Thank you."

"My pleasure." And indeed it had given her pleasure, so much, to be close to animals again. How completely different from her desk job at her parents' furniture store. Idly she wondered if she would ever get the chance to follow her heart back to caring for animals. She scolded herself. Now was not the time to indulge flights of fancy with someone trying to kill her and with her brother in a coma. It was the time to think about business.

"We need to take Pumpkin off the available list for the Camp Town Days. How many horses does that leave?" she said.

"Nine," he said morosely. "Fancy is too old for long rides."

She checked her phone. "We have a party of two scheduled for Tuesday."

He gaped. "We do? Do you think it was the flyers we put out?"

She laughed. "That didn't hurt, but I suspect it was due to the new website."

"What new website?"

She showed him her phone. "I couldn't sleep, and I know how to set up a website since I designed the one for our furniture store. See?"

He flat out goggled at the tiny screen, scrolling through the photo gallery with his thumb. "You did all this last night?"

She nodded.

"Wow."

"Is that a good *wow* or a bad *wow*?" She was shocked at how much she wanted him to be pleased with her efforts.

"It's perfect. I wanted to hire someone to do a website, but I just haven't had the funds to spare."

"Consider it a thank-you for squiring me around everywhere."

"That's not a chore."

Their gazes locked, and she noticed that his eyes were the shade of the deepest summer sky. "Well, anyway, I'm glad you like it." She excused herself from his frank stare. "I'm going to call the hospital and take some aspirin."

"Pain bad?" he said.

She tried for a flirty smile, but her body hurt too much from the wild ride. "I'm okay. Mostly my wrist. Let me know when Jude arrives."

"I think…" he called to her.

"What?"

He looked at the horses while he spoke. "I was just going to say that Seth would be real pleased with the website. I know you don't believe in this place, but I appreciate your effort, anyway."

A wave of emotion swept through her. Thoughts of her brother, pride in her work, happiness that Levi was pleased and sorrow that he was right. She did not, in fact, believe the ranch would succeed. How could it?

Yet as she watched him walk to the house, the low rays of sun wrapped him in the same cocoon of light that dappled the trees and the acres of grazing horses. Levi Duke really did belong here, she thought, on this land, in this place, at this time. Maybe that was really the definition of success, winding up where you belonged.

Stop your daydreaming. She phoned the hospital and talked with her father, decided not to tell him about the danger she'd encountered that afternoon.

"Seth's showing signs of increased consciousness." Her spirit leaped at her father's words. She could hear the cautious optimism in his tone.

"He's reacting to stimulus, seems agitated at times."

"Oh, let this be the first step to his coming back to us," she managed. Choking back tears, they prayed together. "I'll be there early tomorrow, Dad."

"How's it going on the ranch? I don't suppose you've saved your brother's investment yet?"

She understood his sarcasm. To her own surprise, she found herself offering a defense. "We've actually made progress. There's a new website, and the bookings are picking up."

"Really?"

"Yes, really."

"Hmm. I guess that's two bits of good news, then, today."

"We'll take any good news we can get."

"Amen to that," her father said. "See you tomorrow, baby."

By evening time, Levi felt reassured that Pumpkin Pie would be all right. She'd returned to her normal sanguine self, scarfing down the apple treat he'd offered and relishing the extra rubdown. He was not as confident that it would be smooth sailing through the rest of the Camp Town Days.

He snacked on a slice of leftover pizza while Banjo nosed about in the yard, waiting for Rabbit to appear. The dog didn't realize that Levi had already left the kale offering on the porch during kibble time. Mara was in the cabin, which left him alone to think about next steps.

The website bookings had indeed picked up, and he was not sure how he would keep her safely away from strangers and procure enough horses to meet the need. He missed Seth and his eternal optimism. Had he actually taken advantage of his friend's positive outlook? He'd known Seth would say yes as soon as he'd clapped eyes on the property. But Levi hadn't led him on, had he? He'd made it clear the place was floundering. As least, he hoped he hadn't let his love of the Rocking Horse create too rosy a picture. He was still staring into space when a rumble interrupted his reverie. Levi immediately strode outside.

Mara joined him, and they waited for Austin and Willow to climb out of a truck which pulled a small trailer. Willow carried a bundle under her arm. Their tall frames marked them as siblings, though Willow's hair was strawberry-blond and Austin's a white-blond that shone in the late-afternoon sunlight.

Levi stared at the trailer which held a horse. "What's going on?"

"Well," Willow said, "it seems Hank felt so bad about the shooting on his property and what happened to Seth, he wanted to arrange for you to have Cookie. He said you can pay him whenever you get the funds."

Levi's mouth fell open. "That's too much. I can't…"

"Yes, you can," Willow said, thrusting a bundle into his hands. "Because there's one tiny string attached."

Banjo had left off his rabbit harassment to join them. He immediately set about sniffing at the towel in Levi's grasp.

"What string?" Levi asked in voice rich with trepidation. The bundle began to wriggle, and Banjo went on high alert.

Willow patted her brother on the shoulder. "Since you've got Rabbit and a stray dog, what's one more mouth to feed?"

Levi glanced from his sister to Austin.

"Don't look at me, man. I'm just the labor, and I have plenty of mouths to feed with three dogs already. I'll just get this sweet Cookie into the corral, shall I? See how she does with the others through the fence before we properly introduce them."

Willow giggled. "I'll put the supplies in the house. Looks like Jude is coming." And with that she disappeared through Levi's front door.

Levi peered at the wriggling lump. Jude pulled up behind the trailer. Banjo was on his rear legs, taut with interest about the bundle. Mara gently lifted the cloth to reveal a green-eyed kitten. "A kitten?" Levi hollered to no one in particular. "Why me?"

Jude got out. Banjo was too fixated on the kitten to even bark. "Because you are the Animal Whisperer," Jude explained.

"So you're in on this, too?" Levi demanded.

"Guilty. The kitty was abandoned in a box in the grocery-store parking lot, which is where Hank found it, according to my mom. Mom figured you'd make the perfect Uncle Levi to this cat, and she told Hank as much so he figured he'd toss it in along with the mare. Mom even sent along a litter box and kitty chow so you've got nothing to complain about."

"But..." Before he could get the words out, Banjo lunged forward, snatched the bundle in his mouth and darted to the shade of the porch. Levi ran after him, followed by Mara and Jude.

"'Jo, don't hurt him," Levi yelled.

They skidded to a halt to find that Banjo had deposited the mouthful on the porch and was diligently licking the kitten from ears to tail. When it began to mew, he snuggled it up to his belly, tucked a paw protectively over the tiny creature and gave Levi and Mara a satisfied look.

"That beats all," Jude said. "Looks like that

big menace of a dog is the new mommy. It's going to turn out to be the weirdest cat ever."

Mara exhaled in relief. "I guess Banjo wanted to have his own fuzzy family member." They watched for a while until the kitten closed its bitty eyes and slept. The dog relaxed somewhat but remained vigilant.

Levi sighed. "I think people forget I'm supposed to be raising horses, here."

"Nah, folks remember that, too. Everyone who has a busted-down horse they're trying to offload is keeping you in mind, don't you worry." Jude smiled at Levi's groan. "Getting down to business," the sheriff said after a moment, "I got the gist of the little problem you had." He took the jack which Levi had wrapped in a cloth and slid it into a plastic evidence bag. "Unlikely we'll get prints. Talked to Gene. He's upset by the whole thing. Figures you picked up a jack during your kids camp."

"I know what he figures," Levi growled. "You know me, Jude. You know the care I take with my horses. You think I'd miss a metal jack stuck under the saddle? Besides, Pumpkin would have noticed that on the ride over to Gene's. Somebody put it there while we were on his property."

"Your guess?"

Levi shook his head. "Mine would be Teegan."

Mara said, "Mine, too."

"Why?"

Levi shrugged. "His open hostility to Mara. Or maybe Amelia. What do you know about her?"

He tugged his lower lip in thought. "Moved here right after you left, Mara. Same summer, I think. She and Teegan married soon as they turned eighteen."

Mara frowned. "She just looks so uneasy around me, but it might be because her husband doesn't want to talk to me."

"Possible. What are your plans for today?"

"Gonna stick around the ranch," Levi said.

Mara agreed. "We have a couple of tours coming up we need to prep for and the parade on Wednesday."

"And I've got a new equine boarder to settle in," Levi said, rubbing his chin.

"That you do."

"We're going to see Seth in Las Vegas tomorrow. After that, we're meeting Jerry at J and K Excavation." She told Jude about the old appointment book.

"Just to be cautious, I'll meet you there."

"You don't trust Jerry?" Mara asked.

"I don't have any reason not to."

Levi caught the slightest something in his cousin's voice. "But…?"

"But nothing. Jerry's a hard worker, keeps to himself unless it's this time of year."

"The Camp Town Days brings him out of hiding," Levi explained to Mara.

Jude nodded. "Loves the reenactment thing is all. He was an actor back in the day. He's the lead mule-team driver this year. Call me when you're on your way there tomorrow, and I'll meet you." Jude drove away.

Austin emerged from the barn and caught up with Willow as she rejoined Mara and Levi. "Cookie looks right at home," he said. "Sunny is her new best friend."

Mara chuckled. "So Cookie has Sunny, and Banjo has his new cat baby. What are you going to call her?"

Levi shook his head. "I dunno. I haven't even figured out a name for the rabbit yet."

"Better get on that, chief," Willow said.

Mara peered at Banjo and his new charge. "This ranch is getting to be like ground zero for wayward animals."

Willow looked at her sharply. "Levi has one of those exceptional-type hearts, and people around here know that. If you can't share what you have, then why do you have it?"

Her sharpness startled Levi. He was about to reply when Mara answered.

"I didn't mean to imply anything."

Willow paused. "You sure? I know you think this ranch is a money pit and you didn't want your brother to partner in it, but maybe if you got off your high horse, you could see that the ranch is more than an investment."

"Willow…" Levi started, but his sister waved him off.

"I'm sorry. That was rude of me. I'd better go before I say anything else." She kissed Levi. "I'll talk to you soon."

He could feel her tension crackling as she walked briskly past him and drove too quickly off the property.

"Uh…" he started. "Willow is protective of me. I think it's a twin thing. She was born two minutes before me so she thinks she's the alpha."

Mara's look was contemplative. "I deserved it."

He raised an eyebrow.

"Because there's truth in it. I don't want my brother to be your business partner." She paused. "But I'm beginning to think I've been wrong to accuse you of coercing him. You are a good man, and you wouldn't manipulate Seth. I can see why he'd want to jump in to the Rocking Horse. It's…a special place."

Good man? A special place? All sorts of feelings galloped through him at that moment. He was still trying to puzzle over an answer when she finished with "But *special* isn't going to pay the bills." Something like sadness throbbed in her words, which kept the sting of the statement from hurting as deeply as it might have.

He felt a surge of sadness, too. The ranch was indeed the home to lost creatures, castoffs, instead of the thriving horse ranch he knew it could be. Maybe he really was just playing at being a landowner, delaying the inevitable failure of the Rocking Horse.

To his utter surprise, she took his hand, her own fingers silk soft in his calloused palm. "I'll make dinner. I know you want to check on Cookie."

And then he was left standing there with a heart full of angst and a misfit dog bent on mothering a lost kitten. Long rays of gold drifted across the porch announcing the autumn sunset. In spite of his heavy heart, Levi bent his head to thank God for the beauty of the sun sinking into a molten pool across Death Valley.

And then he thanked Him for saving the little discarded cat, too.

NINE

Mara was awakened by the sound of licking. She climbed out of bed to find Banjo administering another assertive tongue-scrub to the yet-unnamed cat. Since Banjo would not go anywhere without his feline charge, they'd moved the litter box and some of the food supplies to her cabin. The kitty peered at her with teeny crystal eyes, seemingly pleased with the attention of her ersatz mother.

Mara showered, dressed in some new clothes Levi had taken her to town to purchase, and set out two bowls, one with kibble and one with kitty chow. It was so amusing to watch both animals eating side by side that she could not help but watch. The kitty ate dainty mouthfuls while Banjo gobbled without seeming to chew. When the kitten had eaten its fill, Banjo helped himself to the remainder of the kitten food.

"Are you supposed to eat food for cats?"

Banjo answered with a happy tail wag. His

exuberance made her laugh. The two followed her to the main house, where she helped herself to coffee and a slice of toast. It was not yet sunup and she heard Levi's low voice soothing the horses as she sat on the porch in the predawn drinking from a chipped mug. The air was crisp, scented with a whiff of alfalfa and fresh-brewed coffee. The Rocking Horse Ranch had its charms, she thought. No doubt about it.

Willow's criticism welled up again.

Maybe if you got off your high horse, you could see that the ranch is more than an investment...

And truth be told, she could see the allure of the land, the satisfaction in being surrounded by horses, the freedom that came with owning a property and tending to it. But that couldn't overshadow the sheer impracticality of it. At least she now realized that she'd made an error in judgment about Levi. Levi invited Seth to join him because he loved the land and her brother.

Willow was right. Levi did have an exceptional-type heart.

If you can't share what you have, then why do you have it?

She pictured her sister Corinne, who had always shared a similar wide-open, risk-taker mentality. Grief and irritation swirled together. Corinne was gone, and Mara, the careful one, was left to support her parents, tend to a store she'd never chosen, redirect her whole life. It hit her that perhaps a tiny part of her anger toward Levi had actually been some jealousy of her brother. Why should Seth dive into his dream life, pull up stakes and live on the Rocking Horse when she was still mired in duty? Jealousy? Why had she not recognized it before? She felt a deep sense of shame.

Her misery flowed unchecked until she took a cleansing breath and prayed it away. "No one forced you to do anything," she reminded herself after the *Amen*. Her decision had been her offering to her parents in the face of the massive hurt they'd experienced. The choice had blessed them, and it was certainly not grounds to dump any residual resentment she might have on Levi. Again she asked for the Lord's grace. From now on, she'd try to help the ranch succeed as best she could and let go of any lingering jealousy.

A lightness fueled her step as she met Levi on the porch.

"Horses okay?"

"Absolutely. Cookie is settled in and eating well. Pumpkin's wound looks good. You treated it perfectly." He took in the dog and his kitty companion curled up under the porch swing. "I gather Banjo is doing well with his mommying duties?"

"Yep. He never lets Tiny out of his sight."

"Is that her name?"

"Best I could do on short notice."

He smiled. "Breakfast?"

"Already ate a piece of toast, and Banjo and Tiny are fed as well. I put out some kale for Rabbit, too."

He laughed. "I'm not used to having a ranch hand around. Anxious to get on the road to the hospital?"

"How did you know?"

"Me, too. Keep a good eye on Tiny, 'Jo," he told the dog.

Banjo waggled his tail, and Tiny mewed.

"I hope he doesn't teach her how to bark," Mara said with a laugh.

They were on the road before sunup. She was not sure if the tingle of tension in her stomach was due to seeing Seth or the meeting with Jerry at his business afterward. For whatever reason, the thirty minute drive seemed to pass slowly, except when she brought up her piece of good news.

"Guess what? A couple emailed via the website. I got them booked."

His smile was effusive. "Really? That's awesome."

"It's for the Saturday parade."

"Well, we agreed to ride our horses in the parade," he said with a frown. "How can we lead a tour also? I don't think I can afford to hire on any guides."

"No need. I told our customers they would be riding in the parade, and then we'll guide them to the Hotsprings Hotel where they're staying."

He quirked a brow. "I never thought to offer a parade ride. That was clever."

"Figured we had to think outside the box."

His admiring gaze made her cheeks go warm. "You're one of the smartest women I've ever met."

The compliment thrilled a deep part of her. She'd heard plenty of praise about her business acumen from the furniture store, but Levi's words struck a louder note in her soul than all those recognitions combined. The warm glow stuck with her until they arrived in Las Vegas.

At the hospital she was so eager to see Seth, she could not get out quick enough, practically jogging to get to the elevator that would take her to her brother's floor. Levi followed along, and they arrived to find several nurses and two doctors in conversation outside Seth's door. The breath caught in her throat as she hurried to them.

"What is it? I'm his sister. What's wrong?"

The closest doctor put a hand on her forearm.

"Nothing wrong. Something right, as a matter of fact. Go on in. I'll check back in a few minutes."

Heart hammering, she pushed inside. Levi stopped behind her in the doorway. Her mother looked up from where she sat at Seth's bedside, her face wet with tears. Her father stood behind her, hand on her shoulder. And then she saw it… the flash of green. Seth's swollen eyes were open halfway. His face was haggard and a ghastly grayish tint, but he was awake.

Tears blurred her vision as she bent to kiss him. "Seth. You're back. I love you so much."

He did not move to touch her or speak until she edged away. He regarded her with a frown. She sent a worried look at her parents.

"Confusion is normal, the doctor said." Her mother could not control the tremble in her voice.

Mara stroked his cheek until at long last recognition dawned in his expression. "Sis," he said.

She laughed and cried and kissed him in her excitement. "Yes, it's me, Seth."

He closed his eyes with a tired nod.

"It will take a while to see—" her mom said "—I mean…to ascertain if there was damage, and to what level he will gain ground."

To what level? She hardly acknowledged the remark. Seth knew who she was, and she believed that deep down he was still her big brother. Eagerly she called Levi over. He came hesitantly, cowboy hat in his hands.

"Hey, man," he said, touching Seth's shoulder. "Welcome back. I've missed you."

Seth's mouth quirked. A smile? A frown? He closed his eyes, and a tear leaked down his cheek. "Levi." His mouth worked as if the words pained him. "The ranch…"

Levi looked stricken. "Don't worry about that. Mara and I have everything handled."

"I'm sorry," Seth said. More tears left wet trails on his face. He closed his eyes again and relaxed into the pillow.

Mara reached to touch him, to urge him to keep talking, but the doctor stepped in. "He may be in and out. Conversations will tire him. Emotions may be all over the place. How about we let him sleep awhile?"

Mara nodded and wiped the tears from Seth's cheeks. "Okay. I love you, Seth," she said. "I have so many things to tell you when you are up to it."

Mara's mother stayed with Seth while her father stepped out into the hallway with them. Levi cleared his throat. "I'm so relieved he's awake, Mr. Castillo."

"We are, too." He paused. "But he seemed agitated, talking to you. The ranch is obviously on his mind."

"Yes, sir. We've got good things to tell him. I—"

"I don't want you to tell him anything." Her father's tone was curt.

"Dad…" Mara started.

Her father's expression was stony. "You think this is all over because he's awake? The doctor's tell me he may need physical therapy, psychiatric evaluation, speech therapy. He may have damage, blood clots, problems swallowing and a raft of other things I can't go into now."

The anger lit her father's normally gentle face.

"Dad," she said again, "Levi isn't to blame for the accident."

"I suppose not," he snapped. "But your brother isn't going to be working a ranch anytime soon. We'll be fortunate if he can return to the same fully independent man he was before. We're blessed to have insurance for this part, but how is Seth going to financially survive a long-term disability since he poured every last cent into your ranch?"

Levi looked suddenly sick. "Mr. Castillo, I'll do anything I can to help. I—"

"You can't help, Levi. Just stay away from Seth. At least you won't be reminding him of his bonehead decision to throw his life savings away."

Levi turned without a word and moved down the hallway.

Mara felt like she'd taken a meat cleaver to the chest. "Dad, I know the ranch wasn't a wise investment, but Levi is a good man, and they both believe in the Rocking Horse Ranch."

"Oh, so he's a good man, now? Before you were furious with Seth for trusting him."

"I know him better since we've been working together. He didn't coerce Seth. They both love the place and thought they could make it work."

"I would have thought one of them might have figured out that was a dumb idea." Her dad fixed her with an iron glare. "Don't get confused, Mara. This whole thing has been a tragedy, and it's far from over. Your brother may never be able to set foot onto this precious ranch. Keep that in mind when you consider what he'll have left to live on."

He turned on his heel. The empty hallway felt cold and desolate. What had been a joyous moment had turned suddenly tragic. What if Seth never recovered fully?

The fear of it froze her limbs for one long moment. There was truth in what her father said. And yet he did not understand what she'd learned the past few days about the Rocking Horse and about Levi. What should she do?

The short-term goal hadn't changed: help the

ranch make it through Camp Town Days. It's what Seth would want her to do, even though her father did not understand. The idea was so much more palatable than it had been when she'd decided on it during her own stint in a hospital bed. She had no idea what Levi would do after she left Furnace Falls. Hurriedly, she made her way to the end of the hallway where he was waiting, shoulders bowed and hands shoved into his pockets.

"I'm sorry about what my dad said… He—"

Levi stopped her with a shake of the head. "Tell him I won't come back."

"But—"

Levi rounded on her. "And maybe you shouldn't come back to the Rocking Horse, either."

Mara stopped short. "Is that what you want?"

He scrubbed a hand around his close-cut hair. "None of this is what I want. Not one thing."

In the truck, Levi was hoping Mara wouldn't have anything else to say about what had happened with her father. A brick of regret and guilt settled into his gut as he dutifully phoned Jude and told him they were on their way to J and K Excavation.

"You okay?" Jude inquired.

"Sure. See you soon." Levi could not seem to force any enthusiasm into his voice. He'd been stupid, naive, to think Seth would wake up good as new. He'd never even considered the possibility of extensive damage.

How is Seth going to financially survive a long-term disability since he poured every last cent into your ranch?

He'd ruined his friend. The reality of it weighed heavily. What could he do? There was only one solution. Sell the ranch and give whatever he could get to Seth. It wouldn't recoup full price, but it would be something. He fought a swell of pure despair.

On the heels of that thought came another even more painful one. When the ranch was sold, Mara would leave for good. He forced himself not to look at her in the passenger seat. Her smile, her laugh, her love for her family. She would be taken away from him like his beloved ranch. The realization awakened an ache deep inside him unlike anything he'd ever experienced. But there was no other way. Might as well get used to it now. At that moment, something shuttered inside him as if he'd crept back into some dark room where no light could penetrate.

Get through the next week. Do what you have to do for Seth.

Mara reached out and touched his shoulder.

"My father is upset, worried. He shouldn't have talked to you like that."

He forced himself to stare at the road. "Mara, I won't let Seth struggle. I'll make it right, I promise."

"What do you mean?"

"Doesn't matter. I'll do it. You should be with Seth. I can get Austin and Willow to help with the tours we've scheduled. It's okay for you to leave."

To his surprise, she poked him in the shoulder. "Levi Duke, you should know by now that I don't run away from my commitments. I said I would help you get through Camp Town Days, and I meant it. We'll bring in some cash, help you pay for Cookie, and that will give you some breathing room."

"Seth needs you," he insisted.

She folded her arms across her chest. "News flash. You don't get to tell me what my brother needs. I have taken care of my parents since you two enlisted and then when my sister ran away. Do you know what it was like to go through the months of searching? Every phone call, every moment, we waited for news."

He wanted to apologize, but he couldn't get a word out.

"I will take good care of my brother by helping you, and don't you dare imply that I don't know what's best for him."

He saw the glitter of tears. "I didn't mean to."

"Then, don't," she snapped.

He let out a long, slow breath and took her hand. Her fingers slid between his, and he squeezed them gently. "I'm sorry. You are a strong person," he said, bringing her knuckles to his lips and kissing them. "It's been a huge amount on you with your sister, now Seth…and some killer stalking you. I apologize if I sounded like I was bossing you."

She didn't answer, but she tightened her grasp for just a moment before removing herself from his. Valiantly, she blinked the tears away.

He resolved not to add to her burdens with his decision to sell the ranch. What they needed to do now was find an explanation for the strange text Mara had received so she could put Corinne's death out of her mind. As he drove along the twisting road to Jerry's shop, he prayed that he could at least help her with that.

TEN

Mara took in the sprawling patch of graveled land that was J and K Excavation. A trailer next to a towering pile of dirt sported an *Office* sign. Across the lot was a neat, wood-sided house which had to be Jerry's residence. Jerry even had a bunch of potted cactus and a cluster of Joshua trees shading his front yard. The area was still, the backhoe parked near the trailer along with various machinery waiting for the next job.

"Jude will be here in ten minutes," Levi said. "We should wait."

But Jerry must have spotted them because he pushed open the front door of the trailer and beckoned them inside. Might as well get it over with, Mara figured as she climbed out. As she started into the trailer a step ahead of Levi, she smiled at Jerry. "Jude Duke will be joining us. Hope you don't mind."

Jerry's eyebrows elevated. "Oh, sure. No problem. I'm expecting a visitor in a few minutes back at the house, so I'll just own up to this mess and let you have at it."

A dirty skylight dome revealed the chaos. The bookshelves on the far wall had no doubt collapsed due to their heavy load. Cardboard boxes disgorged stacks of papers onto the floor. Old hardbound books were scattered here and there in the mess, and an entire shelf worth of files covered the floor. Jerry sighed. "I've been trying to shove everything into piles, but it isn't the top of the priority list, you know? Fortunately, my desk is on the other side of the room."

His small desk was also cluttered with papers in a teetering inbox, with barely enough room on the surface to house a phone. "Pretty quiet around here since we're closed on Sunday, so take your time." He winked. "Now, I'm not expecting you to clean up this mess, but if you want to make piles I would not refuse you."

Mara nodded. "Thank you."

"I'll be in the house if you need anything. Like I said, the appointment book is a green spiral-bound thing about as big as a pastrami sandwich."

He exited.

Mara looked around the mess. "The phrase 'needle in a haystack' comes to mind."

Levi nodded. He went to the front window. "I

can see the road from here so we'll know if Jude or anyone else approaches that way."

"Expecting trouble?"

He answered with a shrug. She went to the nearest mound of files and began to thumb through them before piling them into one of the empty boxes. She thought back to the message she'd gotten on her cell phone. *Marbles.* It had to be some sort of strange coincidence, and no doubt they were wasting valuable time, yet some urge kept her scanning files until one caught her attention.

"Hmm."

Levi joined her. "Find something?"

"Not the appointment book, but a bid on a project to pour a small concrete patio." Her gaze met Levi's. "At Teegan's house."

"Date?"

"That part's torn off. This is just an estimate for the bid. Doesn't really prove anything, I guess. But it is a connection between Jerry and Teegan."

She began to root around in earnest. "If we could just find that appointment book and pin down his location around the time I got that text… It won't explain what happened, but it might be a step in the right direction."

The rumble of an engine starting up vibrated the trailer.

"I thought they didn't work on Sundays?" Mara said, but Levi was already hurrying toward the trailer door to get a better look. He'd no more pushed it open than the trailer shook, her scream drowned out by the creak of the structure toppling over.

Levi struggled to regain his footing as the floor of the trailer buckled. He was pitched hard onto his knees. In a moment, the window fractured, and rivers of dirt began to flood through. The trailer was knocked from its footings and tilted backward, tossing everything in a tumultuous cascade toward the rear.

"Mara!" he shouted. He could not see her through the cloud of debris. He pushed to his feet only to be knocked over again by a second wave of dirt. When he righted himself, the trailer seemed to have settled onto its back wall. Scooping armfuls of dirt out of his way, he plowed toward the corner where he'd last seen Mara.

He made out an edge of the crumpled bookshelf and shouted for her again. Another onslaught of moving detritus drowned out anything else, and he had to wait for it to subside. He tried again.

"Over here," came the answer.

His soul burgeoned with thankfulness. "Where exactly?"

"I'm not sure. I can't see anything but dirt."

"Hold on. I'm coming for you."

"Levi," Jude crawled through the door now in the ceiling which had been the floor moments before.

"Mara's buried. Help me."

"Here," Jerry called, thrusting a small spade through the opening to Jude, who passed it to Levi. "Backhoe's turned over so I can't use it to dig out. We're going to have to do it the hard way. She alive?"

"Yes," Levi all but shouted. His angry questions about how exactly the destruction had occurred could wait until he got her clear. He plunged the spade into the pile, but it caused more debris to settle and move.

"Stop," Mara shouted. "That's making things worse. There's a space here, a little dome thingy. Maybe I can get out that way."

He realized she must be talking about the skylight. "Hold on. I'll clear it from the outside."

He climbed back up after Jude, out the door opening and across the half-crushed trailer. The spot where the skylight should be was covered but not completely. He set to work with the spade, and Jerry and Jude joined in with shovels. At first it seemed that their progress was as quickly erased as they made it, but finally they began to move enough earth that the skylight came into view. Mara's face peered up at them from the inside.

"It's caught," Levi said. "I'm going to pry it loose."

He and Jude grabbed the edge of the skylight and yanked on it. Sweat beaded Levi's face. At first the domed pane refused to budge. Slowly, ever so slowly, the plastic gave until it cracked in the middle. Levi tore off half the broken piece and they worked on the other half until it was bent out of the way.

He lay on his stomach and stretched down to Mara. Her fingertips were a good six inches from his.

"I can't reach," she called.

He groaned in frustration.

"I'll hang on to you." Jude took hold of Levi's belt. The extra distance was enough. He caught Mara around the wrists and held tight.

"Haul me out," he grunted to Jude.

Jude and Jerry eased Levi from the hole, Mara sliding out just enough. Another set of hands joined in to guide Mara free. *Teegan*, Levi thought with fury, staring at the young man. Ignoring Teegan, he moved Mara away and settled her on an overturned bucket, well away from the ruined trailer.

Levi bent to Mara. She was filthy, her hair clumped with dirt, eyes gleaming against the dark soot covering her face. He stroked her hair, anyway, thankful beyond measure that she appeared to be unharmed.

She blinked, coughed, blinked again.

"Are you hurt?"

She wiped dirt from her forehead. "No, just sort of stunned. What happened?"

They took in the scene. The backhoe was half-buried and on its side, engine still running until Jerry jogged over and cut the motor. He stood, hands on hips, looking at it before he trudged back to them. "I can't understand it. Someone wrecked my office on purpose."

"And almost killed two people," Jude reminded him. He swiveled a glance to Teegan. "Mind if I ask what you're doing here on the property?"

Teegan bristled. "I just drove up. I was supposed to meet Jerry to talk about the announcements he's making after the parade about the vendor fair. I got here just in time to see a big old pile of dirt rise into the air. Before you ask, I didn't see who was driving the backhoe."

"And you?" Jude put his next question to Jerry.

"I was fixing myself a sandwich in the house

waiting for Teegan when I heard the backhoe start up. We leave the keys in it. Couldn't figure out who would have fired her up since we're closed Sunday, so I ran out. Like Teegan, I didn't see the driver. It looked like a war zone by that time."

Jude asked a few more questions. "I'm going to check the property. Mara, do you need an ambulance?"

She shook her head wearily. "I feel like I get that question a lot lately. No, I am okay."

Jude headed off between piles of gravel and stacked pallets.

Jerry brought bottles of water from the house for Mara and Levi. Mara drank deeply.

"I feel just terrible about all this," Jerry said. "Did you even find what you were looking for?"

"No." Mara's gaze went to Teegan. "But I saw an invoice that you were bidding on a project for Teegan."

Teegan's eyes narrowed. "Yeah? So what? We wanted a back patio poured for Peter so he could ride his bike."

"I wrote up the bid, but we didn't do the work," Jerry said, wiping at a yellow splotch on his shirt.

Teegan shrugged. "Too expensive. It's going to have to wait a while. Why is that your business, Mara?"

"I got a text from Jerry's phone on October

twenty-eighth, possibly by someone impersonating my sister."

He gaped. "Corinne? She's dead."

Mara cocked her head. "Presumed. That's why I couldn't figure out how I'd gotten the text. Jerry said maybe someone used his phone."

Levi watched Teegan's expression carefully. His mouth was tight with…fury? Fear?

"I don't see how that's justification for accusing me of what happened here."

"I don't need justification for asking questions," Mara said. The snap in her dark eyes made Levi's nerves thrill. "This is yet another attempt to hurt or kill me. My brother is in the hospital. Someone is out to get my family, and I have the right to be direct."

"That someone isn't me," Teegan said. "I don't know where your message came from or how this mess happened. Your sister is most likely dead, I'm sorry to say. I don't know why anyone would want to pretend otherwise. That's just sick and hurtful." He jammed his hands in his pocket and fished out his keys. "I'm leaving now."

"Jude wants you to stay," Levi said.

"Jude can come find me. I don't have to stand here and take all these accusations." He strode to his car and zoomed away. Jude returned. "No sign of a vehicle. Whoever it was may have ridden in on horseback or walked up from the ravine on foot."

Or driven straight in in his car, Levi thought.

They stayed until Mara had had time to drink more water, and they told him about their conversation with Teegan. As he led her to his vehicle, his thoughts ran wild. The person who'd started up the backhoe had taken a great risk. If it was Teegan, he could have been easily spotted. Same with Jerry. Levi or Mara or even Jude might have noticed whoever it was. The act spoke to a high level of desperation, as did the attack on Mara at the hospital. These were up close and personal attacks, not just someone shooting from a distance into a car windshield.

Mara was examining the scene, too, as they walked by Jerry's office.

"Could have just as easily been Jerry," Levi mused aloud. "He could have fired up the backhoe before Teegan arrived and pretended he was making a sandwich."

Mara shook her head.

"You don't think so? Why?"

She looked suddenly bashful and beautiful, dirt and all. "Because he had mustard all over his shirt and a smear of it on his chin. That was a man who was enjoying his lunch." She gave him a quick smile. "See why I'm not a detective?"

He smiled back, in awe of her ability to even

muster up a grin. "Me neither. I'm glad Jude is responsible for the sleuthing from here on out."

"But I can't help thinking more and more that these threats to my family have something to do with Corinne."

He stayed quiet while she finished her thought.

"Is it possible that someone doesn't want me to know what really happened to her?"

He looked again at the ruined trailer. "I don't know, but from now on we leave it to the police. Agreed?"

After another pained sigh, she nodded. "Agreed."

They made their way back to the Rocking Horse, each lost in their own thoughts. Banjo greeted them in the front drive with Tiny prancing along. In spite of her condition, Mara bent and scratched Banjo and his companion, who both set about sniffing her before she went in search of a shower. He quickly threw on clean clothes and set about his ranch chores, never straying out of sight of Mara's cabin. When he finished, Mara had not yet emerged, but the Duke cavalry had arrived.

Austin and Willow settled at his kitchen table, and so did Jude and Beckett.

"We heard what happened," Beckett said. "What's your take on it, Levi?"

"Could have been Jerry or Teegan or someone else, but it's becoming obvious this is about Corinne."

"Her sister?" Willow said. "I thought she committed suicide or died accidentally in Death Valley."

"That was the official finding," Jude said. "Here's what we know from the archived files. The day before she ran away from home, she called Teegan and wanted to come see him. He admits they talked at length on the phone, and he told her he didn't want anything to do with her. He says she continued to call and message, but he ignored them all. Police were advised of the situation by the Castillos and conducted a search with no results. She may have hitchhiked to Furnace Falls would be my guess. Then nothing. No sign of her anywhere. Two months later, after no clues to her whereabouts, her shoe was found in Death Valley National Park. Dogs were brought in and a search team, but her body and belongings were never found—only the shoe."

"Where?"

"Saline Valley."

Austin frowned. "That's miles of rugged nowhere."

"National Park Service searched for weeks after the shoe was found. Never located her body. They surmised her remains are in a crevice or…well…there might have been some wild-animal involvement," Jude said delicately.

"Is it possible she's alive?" Willow said. "If Mara got that weird text and all…"

Jude shook his head. "I don't want to give any false hope here. She's probably dead."

At that moment, Levi realized that Mara was standing in the doorway, hair glistening with moisture from the shower. From her stricken face, he knew she'd heard Jude's sad proclamation.

"I'm sorry," Jude said as Levi beckoned her in and vacated a chair for her. He caressed her shoulder for a moment, wishing he could ease her pain.

"It's okay." Mara's gulp was audible. "I know that's probably the situation. If Corinne wasn't dead, she would have contacted me somehow and not with some enigmatic message. This text and the postcard are somebody's way of messing with my family—or maybe an attempt to point blame? The question I have now is did she go off into Death Valley and end her own life, or did someone kill her and hide her body?"

"I will go over it again with the park rangers," Jude said. "We'll take a second look while we continue the current investigation."

Mara sighed. "Please, can we keep this from

my parents unless there's something important? They have enough on their plates right now."

"Of course," Jude said. "In the meantime…"

Mara offered a wry grin. "I know. Don't go anywhere alone. Well, I wasn't alone today, and I still nearly got buried."

"My fault," Levi said. "I should have heard the backhoe sooner."

"No," she said, eyes flashing. "It's the fault of whoever tried to bury me under a pile of dirt." She turned a look to Levi. "I'll see you tomorrow morning for the vendor-fair kickoff. Very public. No chance of getting shot, buried or carried off by a horse in the Grange Hall, right?" There was a challenge in her gaze as if she expected him to try and talk her out of it. "Okay, then. I think I'll check emails to see if there are any new reservations and lie down for a while."

"Let me know if you need anything," Levi said.

She turned and went back to the cabin. Banjo jogged after her. When Tiny did not follow quickly enough, Banjo picked her up gently in his massive jaws and carried her into the cabin. Levi watched from the porch until she was safely inside. He returned to the kitchen.

Austin said "I'm going to the vendor fair tomorrow. Another set of eyes on you two."

"Me, too," Willow said. "No one pays any attention to the photographer, so I'm going to focus on Teegan and Jerry, too, if he's there. Anyone who seems to linger around you or Mara."

Beckett nodded. "I'll talk to Herm. He was born here in Furnace Falls, and he's been cooking for our hotel for twenty-plus years. He knows everything about everyone. I'll get his perspective on Teegan and Amelia."

"Now, go take a shower," Austin said to Levi. "You look like a mole just come up for some fresh air."

Levi thanked them as they left. Willow lingered behind.

Willow looked thoughtful. "Mara's tough. I like that."

"Yes."

"And she loves her family. Maybe I've been too hard on her. She does have some good qualities."

The best, Levi thought. He realized he was staring in the direction Mara had taken like some sort of starry-eyed puppy. Willow's eyes narrowed. "Levi? You aren't falling for Mara, are you? I know you had a thing for her our senior year."

"What?" He felt heat burning him from the inside out. "We're just working Camp Town Days together, that's all."

She arched an eyebrow. "You sure that's all?"

"Yes. It's only for a week."

And then he would sell—it was the right thing to do.

And then he would say goodbye to Mara.

Why did that feel like he'd been handed a prison sentence?

ELEVEN

Mara let herself into the main house since Levi made it clear that the kitchen was hers for anything she needed. What she desperately required was coffee, and plenty of it, since she had tossed and turned all night in the tiny cabin cot. She was already on her second cup when Levi returned from feeding the herd, clomping through the front door. There was the look she'd seen before, the soft contentment that overtook him after he'd been working with his horses. She imagined the same look shone on her face when she was interacting with animals. She took a large swallow of coffee that burned her mouth.

"All set for tomorrow?" she said. "The Johnsons confirmed for the Death Valley excursion. We'll drop them at their campsite on Gene's property at the end. I'm hoping we can get some good pictures of happy customers and post them to our website gallery."

He nodded. "Since I know you're going to insist on being there, Austin is coming along for some extra protection."

"Better him than Willow." Mara frowned. "She's not my biggest fan, is she?"

Levi drank some coffee from the mug she handed him. "She's coming around. How's Seth?"

"He's still confused. Mom said he's very emotional, which isn't uncommon after a head injury, and the doctors are watching carefully. They are pleased with his progress."

The comment evoked a painful expression from Levi. He stood with his back to her, staring out the small kitchen window.

She put her hand on his shoulder. "Levi, I know you're still thinking about what Dad said. Seth will be okay, no matter how the ranch does."

He looked over at her hand touching him, and he slowly turned to her. His sorrow was so palpable she could not understand how she had ever thought he was using her brother. This was a gentle man, a selfless man, who would not ever stoop to manipulation.

"I know," she said softly, "that Seth would have loved to be a part of this. Good business or not. I think some of my reaction was plain old jealousy."

He blinked at her. "Jealousy? Of this place? Why?"

Should she tell him? It was a level of intimacy that she had not revealed to anyone. After a breath, she said, "Corinne and I argued on her last night at home. She wanted to go back to Furnace Falls, and she was complaining. It was all she did since we'd moved, and it got worse after Seth enlisted. Complain, sulk, go silent. I finally couldn't stand it, and I snapped and told her to stop being a selfish brat."

"And she ran away so you felt guilty. It's why you dropped vet-tech school and went to work for your parents, isn't it?"

Pain twisted her insides. "It sounds so simple when you say it, but Levi, my last words to my sister were terrible. My parents never expected me to work at the store, to give up what I wanted, but it was my way of making amends, I guess. I assigned myself the role. When I look around here, at this ranch, I feel like this is freedom for Seth, like he was embarking on a dream life when I gave up mine. Dumb, huh? My choices, not anybody else's."

He slipped a hand under her chin and tipped her face to his. "Not dumb. I understand that completely."

And she saw that he did indeed understand, without judgment, without condemnation. It lit a beautiful flame inside her soul. "You're the only one I've ever told that to."

He smiled. "Then, I am honored. You are one of a kind, Mara."

She could not continue to hold his thick-lashed gaze. "One-of-a-kind people don't call their sister names or develop a martyr syndrome like I have," she mumbled to the floorboards.

"Yes," he said slowly, "they do. We all fall short. We all need grace. Don't let yourself live in a cage of guilt. You have too much to give to the world."

His lips were so near hers. The heady scent of his soap swirled in her senses. "I will try," she whispered. "But only if you try, too. Your ranch did not ruin my brother, and you are not responsible for saving him."

Levi tried to look away, but now it was her that put a finger to turn his face back to hers. "Promise you'll try."

He bent just close enough that she heard his murmured reply. "All right. I will. For you."

"For us," she murmured, as his lips grazed her cheek.

Had she really said that aloud? There was no *us*. What would he think? Before she could make light of her comment or change the subject, he kissed her temple, and she found herself wrapped in his strong embrace. For one long and precious moment, she rested there, and their connection was so sweet, so natural—it felt perfect.

But what was she doing? In a week, she would be gone, with or without answers about her sister. She'd have to return to Henderson to run the store, perhaps to care for Seth wherever he might be sent for the best care. Whatever she'd found here in the desert would be a memory.

She withdrew from him, and he let her go easily enough. That hurt most of all. It told her that he did not share the strange emotions that passed through her while in his embrace. And there was something, in his posture, in the dullness of his eyes, that made her feel like he had some plan afoot, something that pained him to think about. And she'd added to that pain, unwittingly. So it was her duty to restore the distance between them.

Duty, Mara. It always comes back to that.

"I'll grab my bag, and we can go," she said.

He didn't reply, but she felt his heavy gaze on her as she turned away. She'd gotten a few steps when he stopped her.

"Mara?"

She faced him. "Yes?"

There was a puzzled crease on his forehead, as if he was trying to resolve a problem. "Never mind."

She wondered what he had been about to say. Something tender? No, more likely something practical. That was their relationship. Temporary partners on the Rocking Horse Ranch. And that's all she wanted, wasn't it?

Levi's stomach simply would not relax as they drove to the Grange Hall. Likely it was tension about the upcoming crowd they would encounter. Mara's safety should be occupying his thoughts, not the way her skin felt against her cheek, not the promise he'd made.

For us...

Us. He'd never really dreamed of an *us* with anyone else except for Mara. Though he would not admit it even if he was being drawn and quartered, he'd spent more than his share of time over the years imagining being Mara's one and only. She was just...different from other women. Down to earth, her values in line with his, the way she just plain sparkled, made up for his clumsy conversation, sharpened his dull corners. He was a window, and she was the light that passed through and illuminated everything.

"Sweetie."

The word broke into his reverie. "Huh?"

"Mrs. Johnson isn't an experienced rider like her husband, so I was thinking of Sweetie for her tomorrow."

Business. Why don't you try putting your mind on it? Maybe he'd catch a break, and one of the customers would be a wealthy businessperson looking to buy a dumpy old ranch. "Sure. Sweetie would be great."

They parked in the reserved slot, and he grabbed the bundle of flyers. Mara toted a bag she'd brought, and they entered the Grange Hall. The big room had been transformed. There were bales of hay stacked in corners and decorated with saddles. Tables covered in checkered cloths lined the space. Some had already been festooned with wares: candles, old-time photographs, beaded necklaces, honey, homemade jams, jellies and pies. The reenactment group had somehow managed to get a small replica of a mule-team wagon into the space, and their people were in costume, bustling around with displays about Borax mining and information about how to get a spot in camp on Gene's property.

"Ten. That's our table," Mara said. He stuck close by her side as they meandered through the people. He intended to plop the Rocking Horse Ranch flyers on the table, but Mara had other ideas. From her bag, she took old horseshoes and the ranch photo she'd borrowed from the wall of her cabin. In a matter of moments, she'd set up an eye-catching display, complete with a clipboard for folks who wanted to sign up for their newsletter.

"We have a newsletter?"

She laughed. "You will before I leave."

He wanted to tell her then that he'd decided to sell the Rocking Horse, but her glow of enthusiasm was so sweet he could not bring himself to say it. It would likely take several months to complete any transfer of property, anyway. Surely it wouldn't hurt to bring in some tourist dollars in the meantime. Anything put toward Seth's care would help. But what in the world would they include in a newsletter?

Willow waved at them from across the room where she was taking pictures. Austin would be in the crowd somewhere, too. Their presence brought him comfort, knowing he was not the only one watching out for Mara.

Gene approached, in a plaid shirt, baggy jeans and suspenders. "That display looks very inviting," he said. "Nice touch with the horseshoes."

"Thank you," Mara said.

"Like what you see?" Gene waved a hand around.

"Yes. The planning team did a great job."

"Hours of work, for sure." Gene's smile dimmed. "Look, I'm not sure how to say this, but I heard you accused Teegan of the accident at the J and K."

"It wasn't an accident," Levi said. "Just like the jack under my horse's saddle wasn't."

He pursed his lips. "I'm inclined to come around to your way of thinking. Too much trouble cropping up to be pure accidents, but—" he cleared his throat "—I want you to know that Teegan isn't capable of that kind of thing. He's a gentle man. When my wife died…" He swallowed. "She died of cancer when he was a young teen, and it killed him an inch at a time to see her suffer. Killed all of us, but Teegan took it hard. Felt like he tumbled into a well, and I couldn't drag him out because I was grieving, too. That kind of loneliness can blacken someone's soul, but it didn't with Teegan. I am grateful that he came out of it and got himself a wife and a son. Family's the only thing that can save a man."

Mara hesitated. "We didn't accuse him. We're trying to figure out if any of what's happened is connected to my sister Corinne's disappearance."

His eyes widened. "Your sister? But that was almost five years ago. What would it have to do with the present?"

"Good question," Levi said.

His attention wandered to Teegan, who had hoisted his son onto his shoulders. Both were smiling. Amelia sat behind her watercolor booth, gazing up adoringly. "Teegan's a good man and a good father. Much better than I ever was. I'd do anything for him."

Someone called out to Gene, and he waved. When he turned back to them, his face was troubled. "Truth is I'm a simple man. Not savvy about investigations and police matters and such, but I can tell you without doubt that Teegan did not hurt your sister and he did not cause any of these troubles for you and your brother."

Mara nodded. "I appreciate you coming to talk to me."

"Sure. I'm glad to have this all cleared up." Gene left, stopping to give his grandson a tickle. Teegan noticed Mara. His grin vanished, and he lifted the boy down and handed him to Amelia. Then he turned away.

"Do you believe Gene?" Mara asked Levi. "That Teegan is innocent of any wrongdoing?"

"Seems like Gene believes it, but he said he'd do anything for his son so he might know something he's not willing to come clean about, to cover for him." Levi realized he was tense, muscles rigid. He didn't know anymore who to trust.

Yes, he did. Family. Willow, Austin, Beckett, Jude, Seth…and Mara.

He tried to hold on to that surety as the morning rolled into noontime. Mara stood and stretched. "I'm going to look around at the booths. The flyers can take care of themselves for a few minutes."

Levi didn't ask permission, he simply sidled up next to her, and they began their rounds. Hard as it was to believe, someone had shot Seth and attacked Mara, someone who could be any one of these jolly, bearded participants.

Mara admired a necklace which held a tiny bottle filled with Death Valley sand.

"If you want sand, I got plenty over at the ranch," he said. She laughed, but when she and Willow went to use the ladies' room, he bought it for her and slid it into his pocket. Would he ever have the courage to give it to her? Willow snapped a picture of him standing next to a pile of woven blankets, arms crossed.

"You look like some sort of cowboy secret service agent."

He shrugged, realizing that every minute Mara was out of his sight was a minute too long. *Just doing it for Seth*, he reminded himself, but the sentiment rang hollow. When Mara rejoined him, they kept on perusing the various vendors until they reached Amelia's table. Crates of small watercolor paintings cluttered the surface. Amelia chatted amiably with a customer as she bagged up their purchase.

When she noticed Mara and Levi, she seemed to shrink a little. "Hello. How's business at your table?"

"Lots of visitors," Levi said. "Yours?"

She shrugged. "Okay, I guess."

Levi noticed Peter playing underneath the table. "You've got a helper."

Amelia squirmed and stepped closer as if to shield her son from them. "My husband wouldn't like us talking here, especially after what you said to him at Jerry's."

"Just looking," he said. "But if it makes you uncomfortable..."

A gasp from Mara brought him up short. She was flat out staring at a small painting in one of the crates. He looked closer. It didn't look like much to him. Truthfully, it was more crudely done than the others, at least to his unpracticed eye. Mara bent to scan it more closely.

"This painting. It's yours?" she asked Amelia.

Amelia picked it up. "No. Weird. Mine are much better. I don't know how it got into my stacks."

It was an attempt at a landscape, a depiction of a twisted rock formation. Overhead was a cloud shaped like...

"A teapot," Mara said, exhaling. "How can you not know where this painting came from?"

She looked helpless. "Honestly, I don't know. We've done a few local events. Maybe another artist's got mixed up with mine."

Excitement radiated off Mara in waves. "There's no signature. And I don't see any others like it."

Amelia said sharply "That must be what happened. It's the only explanation."

"I want to buy it," Mara said at last.

Amelia shook her head. "No. It's not for sale. I wouldn't feel right selling someone else's work."

"Please."

"Why?" she said warily. "Why would you want it? It's not very well done."

"It reminds me of my childhood. I'll give you a hundred dollars for it." Her cheeks were flushed.

Levi was stunned at the generous sum, but he knew Mara was privy to something he wasn't. She was almost feverish.

Amelia thought it over. She looked around quickly, perhaps to see if her husband was watching. "Okay." Speedily she stuck the painting in a bag and handed it to Mara, sliding her credit card on the handheld machine.

Mara thanked her and practically pulled Levi back to their table. "Willow, can you watch our table for a minute? I need to show Levi something."

Willow sat down at the booth's table. Her expression was alive with curiosity as she picked up on Mara's mood. "As long as I get to hear about it, too."

"Promise," Mara said as Willow settled onto the card chair. Levi didn't need any urging to follow Mara outside. The parking lot was almost full, but there were hardly any people around.

They sought the shade of a tree on the edge of the lot where she unbagged the painting.

"Are you ready for a bombshell?" she asked.

He straightened. "Lay it on me."

"I think my sister painted this."

Her sister, Corinne, back from the dead.

TWELVE

Mara didn't wait for Levi's questions. "The cloud, see? Right above this four-pointed mountain?" She stabbed a finger at the white blob. "You thought it looked like a teapot, didn't you?"

He nodded.

She rushed on. "That's a long-standing family joke. Seth and Corinne and I would lie on our backs and look up at the clouds. We'd imagine all sorts of fanciful shapes, animals and castles and such, and my brother would always say 'I only see a teapot.'"

Levi stared from her to the painting. "Well…"

"Corinne painted this," she insisted. Her mind was spinning out the theory faster than her mouth could keep up. "Maybe she's alive, Levi, right here in Furnace Falls. Teegan's keeping her prisoner or something, all these years. That's why she didn't call. He's kept her locked up."

"Hold on a second. You might be getting

ahead of yourself. It could be that the cloud just happens to resemble a teapot."

"No. You see the handle here and the spout?" She pointed, amazed that he would even suggest such a thing. "It's deliberate, a kind of message, I'm sure of it. My sister might have heard somehow that Seth and I were coming to Death Valley for Camp Town Days, and she was trying to send us a message, like the text, but she had to be careful not to be caught."

He frowned. "Seems far-fetched to think you or Seth would actually spot this one tiny painting. What are the chances—"

"It must have been all she could do."

He held up a palm to stop her rebuttal. "Mara, slow down a minute. Let's say your sister did paint this, and somehow it turned up in Amelia's things. If Teegan had something to do with holding her prisoner, he sure wouldn't have given her paints. And if you're right, and this is Corinne's work, isn't it possible she painted it years ago before her disappearance? Might it have been in a box of old things or something? Maybe she gave it to Teegan when they were in high school, and he forgot about it?"

Mara's excitement began to ebb. "I didn't think of that."

"I sure don't want to crush your hopes, Mara, but you heard what Jude said."

"That she's dead." Mara blinked back sudden tears. "But they never found her body. I didn't realize how I was hanging on to that part." If they didn't find her body…there was the slightest possibility that Corinne might be alive. The painting had brought that slender thread rocketing to the surface. For a moment, she'd felt a surge of wild, impractical hope, like she'd experienced in the weeks after Corinne disappeared when there would be a call or a knock at the door.

She's come back.

My sister.

But the knocks and calls had never panned out. And Levi was right: this painting was probably nothing, either. How had she come up with such a wild theory in the space of a few minutes? She felt foolish. Her cheeks were wet, and she hadn't even known she was crying.

Levi hugged her close. "I'm sorry, Mara. Likely I'm wrong."

She sniffled and wrapped her arms around his waist. "No. I was being stupid."

"Maybe not. What do I know, anyway? I agree it was weird that Amelia didn't know how it got into her collection and the picture reminds you of your past. I'm not sure it amounts to proof your sister is alive is all. I just don't want to see you hurt."

She buried her damp face against his shirt,

loving him for trying to comfort her. Loving him? She thrust the thought away. "It's okay. For a minute, I wanted to believe it so badly."

"I get it." He held her close and laid his cheek onto the crown of her head. He rocked her there in the circle of his arms, the rough fabric of his shirt whisking her cheek. Though she had no right to, she clung to him for comfort.

"With Seth's situation so unsettled," he murmured, "it's bound to ratchet everything up to a high level."

She squeezed him close and then pulled in a deep breath. Slowly her senses seemed to come back online. Wiping her eyes, she straightened out of his embrace.

They looked again at the painting, and she sighed. "I'm glad I bought it, anyway. It was nice thinking about Seth and his silly teapot clouds. I'll show it to him and remind him about that memory next time I see him." She tried to inject some strength in her words, but she still felt ridiculous and depleted.

"Is there anything written on the back?" Levi asked.

She turned it over. Nothing but a smudge of brown paint. "No."

"We'll show it to Jude. See what he thinks."

She knew he was trying to help her feel less of a fool. After another steadying breath, she said, "I guess I should go explain to Willow that I jumped to a highly improbable conclusion."

"She won't judge you for that. She loves her siblings as much as you do yours."

My siblings, she thought miserably. One dead and one in the hospital in who-knew-what condition. She shook her head to clear away the self-pity. "I'll leave it in your truck for safekeeping."

He unlocked the truck, and she slid it under the passenger seat, out of sight of anyone who might be looking, and they returned to the Grange Hall. Willow looked up expectantly, and Mara's face went hot. Quick as she could, she whispered an abbreviated explanation to Willow. She was surprised when Willow took her hand and gave it a firm squeeze.

"I'm sorry," she said. "If anything happened to Levi or Austin, I would have grasped at any straw, too. Don't feel silly at all." Their clasped fingers conveyed the sentiment. Whatever animosity Willow had harbored toward her had been forgotten in that precious moment. Mara bit her lip, unable to express her mixture of emotions. And all of a sudden, she felt as if she might have a new friend in Willow, or at least an ally.

During the remaining hours, she plastered on a smile, greeting passersby and trying to keep from looking at Amelia. The space began to get stuffy, and her back felt sticky with perspiration.

A dozen or so people signed up for the Rocking Horse Ranch newsletter, which cheered her. Others stopped to get flyers, and they added a pair of sisters to the Johnson tour. Perhaps they might be convinced to provide some testimonials she could use in the newsletter she intended to start work on later that day.

Finally, as the vendor fair came to a close, Levi helped her cover the table. They would leave the flyers and a fresh sign-up sheet, even though they would not be manning the table anymore due to their tour activities. She grabbed her bag. Levi opened the door to the parking lot, and she followed him.

There was a tinkling of glass. It took them both a moment to identify the sound.

Though Levi's truck was hidden by a row of other cars, somehow she just knew from where the sound had originated. Levi sprinted toward the truck. She grabbed her cell phone, ready to call the police and followed after him.

She heard Levi shout "No!" followed by a crash of metal on metal.

Levi got only a vague impression of the vandal, big shirt, hat low on the brow, bandanna over the face before a tire iron was flung at him. He ducked but not quite in time. The tool glanced off his cheek and careened into a parking sign as it sent him over backward.

When the stars cleared, he scrambled to his feet, ignoring the pain radiating through his face. Mara hurried over. "Jude's after him." Her brow crinkled in worry. "You're bleeding."

"I'm okay."

He took the stack of tissues she handed him from her bag and pressed it to his cheek which stung like it was on fire. Tears streamed from the affected eye, and he realized Austin and Willow had emerged from the Grange Hall to join them. Willow insisted he pull the tissues away so she and Mara could examine him. He squashed the mess back to his cheek and tried to wave them off.

Jude returned, breathing hard.

"I chased him around to the front, but they were loading bales of hay for the parade spectators to sit on, and I lost him. Need medical attention, Levi?"

"No," he said quickly before either of the two women could answer for him. "I don't suppose you got a better look at him than I did?" Levi asked hopefully.

"Face was covered. Medium height, baggy clothes. Wearing gloves so I didn't even see his hands. Or hers. Could have been a woman."

They approached Levi's vehicle, and he caught

the gleam of glass, bits of broken pieces lying on the paved surface of the lot.

Jude stood next to Levi's broken passenger window. "All right. Let's hear it. What did you have in there that someone busted your window to get?"

"He didn't leave anything in there. I did." Mara's face was pale. "A painting I bought at the vendor fair, under the passenger's seat."

Jude gingerly slid a gloved hand under the seat. "Nothing there now. What kind of a painting?" he prodded.

She told him about her theory that the piece had been her sister's work. "But I slid that painting all the way under the seat. There's no possibility it was visible. No one could have known it was there unless…"

Levi frowned. "Unless the person who busted in was watching us the whole time."

Watching….the whole time. It made something inside him roll up tight.

"Makes you wonder, doesn't it?" Willow said.

"Wonder what?" Austin asked.

"If there really was some kind of message in that painting Mara bought."

A message…from the grave? What could possibly be going on in this town?

Jude looked at Mara after he finished talking into his radio. "A sheriff will be here in a minute to secure the scene. After he arrives, how about we go have a talk with Amelia and Teegan?"

"Yes," she said calmly. "Let's."

In less than ten minutes, Jude's compatriot arrived. He stayed with the truck while the rest of them returned to the Grange Hall. Levi didn't make direct eye contact with Jude in case his cousin might tell him to stay back while he questioned the Warringtons. There was no way he was going to let Mara go anywhere unless he was glued to her side. Willow and Austin stayed back from Amelia's table, but he knew they were watching curiously. It occurred to Levi that both Teegan and his wife were wearing baggy jeans and loose-fitting shirts.

Teegan stood with his arms crossed and his back to them, speaking to Amelia. They both appeared hot, sweaty. Could one of them have busted into his truck, eluded pursuit and strolled back inside as if nothing had happened? Probably, but the temperature in the hall was climbing, and they'd been packing boxes so everyone was feeling uncomfortably warm, including Levi. Amelia blinked as though she might burst into tears when Jude, Levi and Mara showed up. She broke off from the conversation, cheeks red. "Oh, hi. Did you all need something?"

Teegan was not so solicitous. He wiped a hand over his brow. "What do you want?" he demanded. "I heard you bought some painting that didn't belong to us. Pressured Amelia to sell it to you. What's going on now? Are you back to harass her some more?"

"Teegan," Jude said. "No harassment going on here. You sell art. She bought a piece that reminded her of Corinne. Nothing wrong with that."

"And like I said, she paid well for it, Teegan." There was a petulant quality to Amelia's statement. Levi realized they must have been having a little spat about the sale. "Not like we can't use the money." Her last comment was mumbled.

"Were both of you here for the last thirty minutes or so?" Jude asked.

"Yes," Teegan said, affronted. "Except when we carried boxes to my car. Why? What are we supposed to have done now?"

"Levi's vehicle was broken into," Jude said. "The painting Mara bought from Amelia was stolen."

Amelia blinked. "It was? Who would want it?"

Levi could not decipher any emotion from Teegan. Was he surprised to hear of the break-in? He didn't look it. Maybe he knew already because he'd done it or asked someone else to.

"Did you see anyone loitering around Levi's truck when you were outside?" Jude asked.

"It's not my job to do parking-lot security. That's yours, isn't it?"

No one other than a close friend or cousin likely could have detected the slight tightening of Jude's jaw. His tone remained calm and pleasant. "I didn't catch your answer. You did or did not see anyone loitering around Levi's truck?"

"I did not," Teegan snapped.

Gene came over, cheeks flushed. He held a crate filled with rolls of blank price stickers. "What's going on? What's happened?"

"Nothing, Dad," Teegan snapped again. "Everything is fine. Just cleaning up."

Gene set aside his box to hoist Peter who had crawled out from under the table. Amelia shifted anxiously.

"Hey, buddy," he said, tugging on Peter's baseball cap. "How about Grandpa Gene takes you over to the ice-cream parlor for a scoop?"

Peter held his grandpa tight around the neck and did not look at the adults who were gathered around him.

He stuck his last two fingers in his mouth.

Amelia sighed. "No sucking your fingers, big boy, remember?"

Peter slid them out of his mouth. Teegan said "Dad, go ahead and take Peter now. I'll meet you later at the ice-cream shop."

Gene's eyes were troubled, but he nodded and carried Peter out.

"Are we done here, then, Sheriff?" Teegan asked. "I don't know what happened to this mysterious painting. I never even saw it, so I don't know what you all are talking about. In any case, it's gone, apparently stolen. If you want to buy something else, Mara, come on back tomorrow. Otherwise, we have work to do."

"Thank you for your time," Jude said.

They rejoined Austin and Willow.

"I'm guessing you didn't learn anything?" Willow asked.

Levi nodded. "And without the painting we are sort of stalled again."

"I should have taken a picture of it with my cell phone," Mara said with a groan.

A broad smile dawned across Willow's face. "Hold on a minute." Quickly she opened her bag and clicked through the digital photos in her camera. "Here. I guess it pays off to be nosy."

Levi enjoyed his twin's discomfiture. "You were spying on Mara, weren't you?"

A faint blush tinted her cheeks. "Well, um, yeah, I guess I was. When I saw how interested you both were over at Amelia's table, I just had to find out what you were looking at. I used my telephoto and zoomed in." She offered a wry grin to Mara. "Sorry. My brothers both say I have a curiosity that won't quit."

"Yes," Austin said, "and you exercise it regularly and without restraint. How does Tony stand it?"

"For your information, Tony admires my inquisitive nature, even if he does say I ask more questions than his kids." She cocked her chin. "And in this case, my nosiness might actually be helpful." She held the camera up so they could see the tiny viewfinder. "Look at this shot. You can see Mara holding up the painting in her hand. I can zoom in. The quality won't be awesome, but you can see a little of it. Just a blur of mountain and a smear of white cloud." Her tone sobered. "I guess it isn't really all that helpful, is it?"

Mara grabbed her around the shoulders and hugged her. "It is to me. I was beginning to think I was imagining things. That cloud, blurry as it is, still looks like a teapot. The theft makes me think something is going on, even if it isn't going to lead me to my sister alive and well."

"There is definitely a connection here," said Jude.

"Beckett told me Herm said that Teegan and his dad went into seclusion after his mom died. He actually did some of his high school classwork via a home-study program. Sort of re-emerged six months after her death and met Amelia because her dad was a driver for Gene's trucking company."

"All that jibes with what Gene told us earlier today," Levi said. He tossed the wad of bloody tissues into the wastebasket.

"Oh, Levi. You're going to have such a shiner tomorrow," Willow said.

Levi shrugged. "How is any of this connected? The shooting, the tampering with the saddle, the mess at Jerry's place. I don't get what it has to do with Corinne."

"That's what's been sticking in my craw," Jude said. "I have been studying Corrine's case file in depth. There's nothing that awakens any question except for one thing—why was nothing else found of her belongings? Why not a purse? Her phone? A jacket? Why just the shoe?"

Mara bit her lip, and Levi touched her forearm.

Jude noticed the gesture. "Mara, I feel obligated to say that there is very little to support the notion that your sister is alive. False hope is the worst kind of torture. Like you said, almost five years have passed. The statistics of—"

She stopped him. "You don't need to tell me. I know she's likely dead. If you can find out what actually happened, there will be some peace in that." She looked at the group surrounding her.

"Thank you, all of you, for taking me seriously. I wasn't very gracious about the ranch or coming back here, and you all have been better to me than I deserve."

Levi felt a surge of guilt. Had he taken her seriously enough? He certainly had not jumped on her idea that Corinne had painted the landscape.

There were too many balls spinning in the air for his one-track mind to manage.

His failing ranch.

Seth's fight to come back to health.

Her parents' massive load of worry.

The unaccountable way Mara was becoming twined in his every thought and emotion.

That last realization startled him so much that he tensed, and his hand fell away from her shoulder, leaving a strange sense of loss, as if his body too was beginning to crave her proximity.

What could he do? What should he do? Thoughts thudded in helpless confusion around his brain…except for one.

He had to keep Mara close and safe until Jude could work out what was going on. The emotional chaos should and would be stowed away for later like precisely stacked bales of hay.

With new resolution, he cleared his throat. "Willow, can you drive Mara back to the ranch since my passenger seat is filled with glass? I'll drop my truck at the shop and get a ride back."

"You can borrow my truck while yours is being fixed," Austin offered. "Any excuse for me to ride my motorcycle."

"Sounds good," Willow said, though her frown led Levi to believe she did not think Austin should be riding his motorcycle with his shoulder not fully healed. Like him, she would not hurt his pride by questioning. Willow paused. "Umm, maybe this isn't the time, but are we still going to tackle the Johnson tour tomorrow?"

"No," he said at the exact moment Mara said "Yes."

"We'll cancel." Levi said over her exclamation.

"Oh, no, we won't," she countered.

He went for a logical, even-tempered response. "Things have changed."

Mara flicked her wave of dark hair aside. "Some things haven't. The horses need to be fed, and my brother is going to want to know we did our best. We're doing the tour. We took a deposit, and we have to deliver." She swept off, following a grinning Willow.

Austin looked as though he was smothering a grin as well. "My brother, I think you are about to lose an argument."

"No, I'm not." Anyone would agree that he was right. It was smart; it was common sense.

"Right. Anyway, my schedule is clear for tomorrow so I can go along on the tour as your wingman."

"I said—"

"I know what you said." He winked at Levi. "See you tomorrow, Levi."

Levi climbed into his bashed truck and jammed the engine to life. If she wouldn't listen, then he'd have to tell her he'd decided to sell the Rocking Horse. It was the right thing to do, and no amount of impassioned resistance was going to change his mind. The Dukes did right by people they loved, even when it hurt.

Seth would understand, he had no doubt.

He did not feel quite so confident about Seth's sister.

THIRTEEN

Mara's skull was thumping with a tension headache, but she was too keyed up to sit still at the Rocking Horse. Willow kept her company until Levi returned in Austin's borrowed truck. Willow surprised her with a hug when she left.

"I'm sorry that your picture was stolen."

"At least you got a photo of it. Thank you."

"Good that my nosiness pays off sometimes," she said.

Levi had immediately started in on chores, so Mara decided to make dinner for the two of them. She watched him out the kitchen window as he passed through the fenced corral. Even from afar, she could tell he was unusually somber, filling the horses' troughs with fresh water before stalking around the barn.

She figured he was stewing about her insistence that they carry out the tour. She'd somehow have to explain it to him. To her, it was more than just a tour. The ranch was the only part of her life she seemed able to take hold of. The needs of the place continued on, no matter how her personal life was falling to pieces. There was no danger, really, she felt, as long as she stayed with others and didn't go prowling around on her own asking questions. The burglary of his truck didn't change that. Besides, there was something she desperately had to check out, something she'd seen on the Warrington property that stuck in her mind.

What had changed, she admitted to herself, was the increasing sense that she did not know the whole story behind her sister's death. She'd promised Levi to let go of the guilt over the argument with her sister, and for the most part she'd succeeded, but her spirit was still not at rest. Her growing sadness and unease was pressing with ever-more urgency on her consciousness. The painting, she felt deep in her bones, must have been done by her sister recently, which proved to Mara that she must have come to Teegan's before she drove into Death Valley. Had Teegan killed her, made it look like a suicide?

Pain cut at her. She had an image again of Corinne, her stubborn, bucktoothed little sister. They'd bickered, fought and loved each other deeply. She'd been just beginning to grow into the beauty she would have become when she'd disappeared, her overbite corrected, hair cut into an attractive bob, legs long and athletic.

Mara pulled out a fry pan and set it on the stove to heat. Maybe Teegan was a good father and a good man, like Gene insisted, but if he'd killed Corinne, all of that was null and void, as far as she was concerned. Corinne had been guilty of nothing more than a teen crush on a boy who didn't want her. *What happened to you, Corinne? And who is trying to leave clues for me?*

Her own helplessness buzzed in her nerves. She was not a sleuth or investigator. Would the police put a teen's cold case back on their radar? She trusted Jude enough to believe he would. It was all she could hang on to. It was purely a police matter, except for the one thing she needed to see for herself on Gene's property.

Inserting slices of cheddar between pieces of buttered bread, she set the sandwiches to toast in the hot pan and gathered greens for Rabbit. Banjo and Tiny were occupied chasing each other around the yard, so they would be fed later. Rabbit snuck up to grab the greens while Mara stood there. He was growing used to her presence. Banjo barked from the grass. In spite of her heavy spirit, it made her laugh to see the lug of a dog drop down on his front paws, backside in the air, barking at the tiny cat with the itty-bitty, raised paw.

Willow's earlier comment rose in her memory. *Levi has one of those exceptional-type hearts...* She agreed. Right now, though, she had to deal with his stubborn proclamation that they'd have to cancel the Johnson tour.

When Levi finally joined her in the main house, he washed his hands and sat heavily in the chair, calloused fingers drumming on the table. The bruise on his face was darkening to a livid purple, and his eye was puffy.

Mara decided to dispense with any small talk. "You look ready for battle," she said.

He raised an eyebrow. "Are we gonna have one? I'd rather not if we can avoid it."

"I'd like to avoid one, too, but I am going to help you with that tour tomorrow. Willow said she'll go..." She heard his teeth grind together.

"It's not a matter of how many people are there. Someone's pot has been stirred by things we've done that we don't even understand. There's no way to be protected against a situation like that. Someone is watching, don't you get that?"

"I do," she said calmly. "And I will be careful, but we need the money, and you need the help."

He jammed a finger on the table for emphasis. "Mara, Seth wouldn't want you to do this, to risk yourself, and you know it."

She raised her chin. "Don't you bring my brother into this."

"He's already in this." Exasperation radiated off him. "When I took you out on that date our senior year, do you know what Seth said to me?"

This wasn't at all what she'd expected to hear. She waited.

"Seth said, 'You are the only one on this planet I would trust with my sister.'"

Moisture built in her eyes, and she blinked hard. "I didn't know that."

"I would never be able to look him in the face if I let something bad happen to you."

"He's my brother, Levi," she reminded him. "I know him better than you and he wouldn't want me to sit in a cabin and be afraid of my own shadow and let you struggle to keep this place afloat. Nothing dangerous happened today except your window got broken."

"Things are escalating." He drew out the last word in a way that irritated her.

His eyes flashed. It was so unlike him to be angry that she had to check herself from staring. He was not the kind of man to order people around, either. His ways were quiet, patient, but right now she hardly recognized him. "I'm coming with you."

"No, you're not," he said, enunciating each word.

Her irritation flicked up a notch. "Sorry, but no one put you in charge of me, Levi. I'm here of my own volition, and I make my own decisions."

He was silent for several seconds. "I'm selling it."

The words startled her retort clean out of her head. "Selling what?"

He blew out a breath. "I'm selling the Rocking Horse as soon as Camp Town Days are over. Seth's going to get his money back or at least a chunk of it."

The shock left her immobile. "You can't do that," she finally said. "This ranch is everything to you."

"No," he said slowly, pain showing on his bruised face. Weariness bracketed his mouth in lines. "You and Seth are everything to me. I can't let you scrimp and suffer financially through Seth's recovery because he bankrolled this place on a whim. I can't and I won't."

She could only gape. He was serious. "But... what would you do without the Rocking Horse? Where would you go?"

"I dunno. I'll figure it out. I've been putting out feelers to see who might be interested in taking in the horses. I'd like them to stay together, but that's not going to happen. The older ones will be harder to place. Hank might take Cookie back." His eyes darkened as he stared out the window.

So he'd worked out the whole thing, had he? Without a word to her? Without considering how Seth would feel about it? A trickle of desperate anger ignited in Mara's stomach. From there it started a fire in her heart that flamed out of her mouth before she could stop it. "You are not going to sell this ranch, Levi Duke."

He stared at the tabletop. "Yes, I am," he said, expression flat. "I didn't want to tell you, but there's no point in risking yourself for it now that you know my decision."

"*Your* decision." She glared at him. "Is my brother's name on the deed?"

He finally looked straight at her. "What?"

"Seth is a co-owner of this property, and you need his permission to sell it, even if the paperwork isn't finalized."

He looked at her as if she'd grown a head. "I am making the decision since he's unable to, as you well know."

It took every ounce of effort for her to keep her voice level. "I have power of attorney for Seth until he recovers."

"You're sure of that?"

"Pretty sure." She did remember something of the sort in the trust he'd arranged several years before which would probably render her current pronouncement factual.

"What's the point of this standoff? We're not going to save this ranch."

"Like I said, you don't get to decide that for my brother."

"Mara—" he started, then coughed.

A cloud of acrid smoke made her eyes tear.

"Your sandwiches are on fire," Levi said.

She whirled around. Smoke was pouring from the pan and a bit of cheese had ignited. In a flash she turned off the heat, whacking a lid on the fry pan until the flames were out. Then she dumped his blackened cheese sandwich onto one plate and hers onto another. Plunking it down on the table in front of him, she announced "You're not selling this ranch unless I agree." He opened his mouth to retort, but she gathered her own plate and swooped toward the door so quickly her sandwich almost ended up on the floor.

"And I am going to eat my sandwich in my cabin," she said.

For good measure she slammed the door behind her.

Banjo and Tiny looked up from their game, startled. The animals followed her to her cabin where she thwacked the door shut and plopped down at the table Levi had added for her convenience, staring at the burned mess on the plate in front of her. Fury ballooned to epic proportions. She'd finally accepted that Levi and Seth were partners in good faith, and now Levi was going to sell the ranch right from out of her brother's nose, while he was in the hospital, no less.

"He has no right," she hissed, while Banjo set about licking her ankle for all he was worth. She reached down and patted his head. "Why are men so ridiculous?" she said. "Anyone can see this place is precious."

Precious? What had she just said? The ranch…*precious*? But hadn't she arrived only a few days ago thinking it was the worst idea her brother had ever had to invest here? Both she and her father had been aghast when Seth announced what he'd done. She got up and gazed out the window trying to look objectively.

Fenced acres of gold. Rocks silvered and sparkling. Old horses, new additions. A hawk sitting in the topmost branch of an old pine tree. Everything spoke of age and time and…peace.

It was precious, her heart told her. How had she fallen in love with this small piece of nowhere? A spot of ground that would never be profitable or practical. The sun that warmed her face was like a caress, and she let out a slow breath that took some of her anger with it. Her own feelings aside, the Rocking Horse was a God-blessed place, and she was loath to think of Levi letting go of it. She knew it would rip his heart out and end his dreams and her brother's, too.

Her own reversal of sentiment made her head swim. She'd only recently come to terms with her jealousy sprung from her deferred dreams. Now she was horrified to think that Seth and Levi would lose theirs? She was supposed to be helping keep things temporarily afloat, not watching Levi give up on the place. But maybe he was right... What if her brother did not return to his former vigor? Was he going to be so compromised he wouldn't be able to stay on the ranch? That wasn't Levi's decision to make, she thought stubbornly.

What had been so clear only a week before was now clouded in emotion. She did not want to leave the ranch, but there were more important things at stake than her own daydreams.

At the same time, it took her breath away to think of what Levi was ready to sacrifice.

You and Seth are everything to me. Not just his buddy, his best friend, but her, too.

She had to change Levi's mind, and if it took a legal roadblock, then so be it. But maybe she didn't need to be quite so hardheaded in the meantime. Perhaps she was being foolhardy insisting on helping with the tour at the present time. A plan formed in her mind. She reached for her cell and called Willow to explain.

"And Levi agreed to this?" Willow asked.

"Not yet, but it's a good compromise, right?"

"He didn't look in the compromising mood."

Mara wondered if he had shared with his sister his plans to sell the ranch. She decided not to bring it up. "If he agrees, will you do it?"

"Sure. I have a nighttime tour but not until seven. I'll meet you at the Rocking Horse tomorrow at sunup, unless you call and tell me it's off."

"I won't."

She giggled. "Levi can be stubborn as a mountain when he wants to be."

They disconnected, then Mara splashed water on her face and pulled her hair back. Calm, reasonable conversation was required, no yelling and burning grilled-cheese sandwiches. She opened the door just as Levi's hand was raised to knock.

"Hi," she said, butterflies in her stomach.

"Hi." He grimaced. "No offense, but your grilled-cheese sandwiches are kind of on the well-done side."

A smile crawled across his face as he looked over her shoulder, and she whirled around to see Banjo sitting in the corner with the blackened sandwich in his paws. Tiny was nestled right along with the sandwich, licking the burned bread while Banjo nibbled the corners. The dog looked closely at her, waiting to see if she would take it away.

"At least somebody likes it, but you shouldn't take food off the table, Banjo. It's bad manners."

Levi dragged his eyes to hers. "I'm sorry. I didn't mean to spring that on you about selling the ranch. That didn't come out right."

"It's okay. I shouldn't have blown up. I know you were trying to protect me, and Seth, too."

He looked down at his boots. "If I knew another way…any other way…but there isn't one. I have no other assets except a beat-up old truck. This ranch is all I have worth anything."

"Let's leave it for now, okay? I have an idea about how we can lead the tour tomorrow and still keep things top-security."

He frowned.

She hurried on. "Whether you sell or not, at least it will pay for the feed this week. The horses have to eat, right? And Banjo and Tiny and Rabbit and whatever else you wind up taking in. Will you promise to listen with an open mind?"

He raised a suspicious eyebrow. "I'm too hungry to listen. Can I be open-minded over ice cream? It's all I've got in the freezer since you used up all the bread."

She smiled and folded her arms. "What kind of ice cream, Mr. Duke? I'm not capitulating over some namby-pamby pistachio or rainbow sherbet."

He chuckled, and the light returned to the sparkle in his eyes which, in turn, ignited something inside Mara.

"The only kind worth eating is rocky road," he pronounced.

"You're very arrogant about your ice cream, but fortunately I like that kind."

He looked over her shoulder. "I guess we'll just leave these two to their dinner."

They walked back to the house as the long slanting rays of sunshine turned the dry grass to gold. It was so very hard to believe that someone hiding in those distant, twisting hills had shot her brother, wanted them both dead. Was it all an effort to cover up what he or she had done to Corinne? A cold thrill of fear snaked up her spine, and she was glad for Levi's sturdy house and his comforting presence. She stole a glance at his profile, strong jaw, sensitive mouth, brows so often drawn in thought. Did her growing love of the ranch encompass its rock-solid owner?

But what did it matter? He'd promised Seth to take care of her, and he was bent on doing that. Certainly duty was not the same as love.

Don't get confused, Mara.

She sat while he scooped up two big bowls of ice cream.

"All right," he said, after a couple of spoonfuls. "You said you had a plan. Let's hear it."

"Willow and I will be the sag wagon."

"Come again?" he said.

"You know. A sag wagon follows along after a race with water and supplies and picks up any tired racers, only we'll carry their luggage and camping supplies. Willow already said she'd do that with me. We'll follow along far enough behind that we won't impact the horses."

"But if someone is watching—"

"And this is the best part," she hurried on. "Jude said there is an officer staged along the route, to reassure everyone, mostly."

"How did you find that out?"

"He was visiting Willow when I called. You can't argue with a sheriff ride-along."

"I probably could argue that the safer thing is for you to stay here with someone."

She shrugged. "I believe this is what is called a reasonable compromise."

He cocked his head, the light playing over his strong features. "Why is it so important for you to come, Mara?"

She felt as though he'd seen right through all of her talk to the idea that had been percolating since that afternoon in the Grange Hall. "You'll think I'm being silly."

"No, I won't."

"When I saw the painting with the teapot clouds, it looked like something I'd seen before, when we were at the checkpoint near the campsite on Gene's property." She paused. "That painted mountain, it's such an odd shape, with the four peaks, like a hand with a missing thumb."

He was silent for a full three seconds. "You think whoever painted it was on the Warrington property?"

"Yes." She could only shrug. "Like I said, it probably sounds silly."

He put his palm over her forearm and squeezed. "No, it doesn't."

Gratitude made her suddenly feel like crying. She swallowed hard as he went on.

"I can look. Take pictures. Show it to you."

She shook her head. "I have to go see if for myself, Levi. If the picture is showing something from the Warrington's place, maybe… I mean, maybe there is a slight chance my sister did somehow paint it. It might be some sort of clue about what happened to her. There's a reason it ended up in that box of Amelia's work just when I'd be around to see it. But all the other reasons hold true also. I promised Seth I would help the Rocking Horse through Camp Town Days, and I'm going to do that with as much regard for safety as I can."

"What will happen if you learn nothing? If you go see this place and finish up your time here and leave Furnace Falls and you never find out anything about Corinne? I don't want you to make it any harder on yourself than it has to be."

"What could be harder than thinking all these years that she ran away and killed herself after we'd argued?" Her voice cracked and she gulped.

He went to her, drew her out of her chair and held her close, rocking her gently back and forth. "No guilt," he whispered.

"No guilt," she agreed, "but it hurts so much, as if it was recent, not five years ago."

"Oh, Mara," he murmured. "If I could change things…"

How hard would it be to leave this place, to turn and walk away from Levi, knowing he had given up everything for her and Seth?

His phone rang, and he released her with one hand to check it. He swallowed. "It's a guy who wants to talk about buying the ranch."

"Will you let it go for now?" *For me?* she added silently.

He put the phone back in his pocket and settled his arms around her again. They took their bowls and went to the front porch and sat together, eating ice cream and drinking in a Rocking Horse Ranch sunset.

How hard would it be to see the Rocking Horse sold?

Unbearable, she thought, for both of them.

FOURTEEN

Levi's own reflection dismayed him as he shaved on Tuesday morning. The eye had indeed developed a shiner, and the cheekbone was still swollen. What hurt more was remembering the argument he'd gotten into with Mara the day before. Her reaction had left him as confused as a chameleon in a bag of confetti. All of a sudden, she didn't want him to sell. The irony.

But deep down, part of him was secretly thrilled because he realized the charm of the Rocking Horse was shifting Mara's view on things. Sometimes he'd felt like she'd changed her mind about him, too. He surely was seeing her in a whole different light. Levi was not one for flights of fancy, but for one delicious moment as he dragged the razor over his chin, he wondered what it would be like to have Mara in his life permanently. In his rosy scenario, they'd keep the Rocking Horse, and Seth would join them, too.

The razor stopped in mid-scrape when he realized he'd been imagining her not as a business partner but as a wife. He didn't have that schoolboy crush on Mara anymore. The infatuation seemed to have grown into something deep and tenacious that had him imagining marriage and futures that weren't going to happen. He stared at his reflection, and his daydream evaporated. A guy with a black eye, teetering on the edge of bankruptcy regarded him. A sentimental view of the ranch wouldn't negate the list of problems, old horses, Seth's medical bills, Mara almost killed, the responsible party at large.

The tiny spot of red on his chin appeared before the sting of the razor made itself known. *Get yourself together. Do the tour, and keep Mara safe.* Then he could worry about the other mountain of troubles that awaited. Annoyed with himself, he finished shaving.

He swallowed a couple of aspirin to take the edge off his aches and pains, swigged down with a cup of black coffee. On the counter he found a new package of bread and some bananas along with a note. *I asked Willow to pick up some things on her way here. Truce.*

Truce. He smiled and ate a banana. Mara was already busily packing a cooler with Willow's assistance, and Austin was saddling Cookie. He hurried to help, and they'd gotten six horses saddled, watered and ready when the Johnsons showed up, followed shortly thereafter by an eager-looking pair of sisters, Eve and Doris. All four wore jeans and checked shirts, new handkerchiefs around their necks and cowboy hats fresh from the store. City slickers from bottom to top.

He offered a shy greeting. Mara was already at work chatting with the group and encouraging them to talk to one another. She even discussed general horse care and behavior, which left him awed and grateful. If he didn't have to talk at all, he'd be thrilled. A bond was building between the guests about their upcoming adventure, thanks to her.

Her hair was satiny in the sunshine, eyes dancing as her fingers trailed over Cookie's mane. She'd always been on fire for animals. He recalled her hot pursuit of a wayward tree frog in the high-school lunchroom, desperate to save it from being trampled. After a comical effort, she'd managed to corner it and scoop it up between her palms. Hair disheveled and smiling exuberantly, she'd crooned softly to the little frog as she took it outside. That frog hadn't realized his good fortune to have the most amazing girl in the school save his life.

Greetings over, they assisted the visitors to mount, and he and Austin did the same, leading the group to the cut-through that would take them past town and over to Gene's property and the campground.

The cool autumn morning was magnificent, with the sky a cool washed blue. They cut behind the Hotsprings property, and he made sure to point out its finer qualities. He tried to think of how Mara would phrase things.

"Clean and comfortable, and food can't be beat. Their chef is renowned for his cooking. Well, renowned in Furnace Falls, anyway." As they passed, Laney looked up from leading a couple toward the hot spring that puffed steam into the air. Her old puggish dog, Admiral, was tucked under one arm, and Beckett was close to her side. He'd pretty much been that way every day since she'd almost been killed and he'd been exonerated as a serial killer. Her sleeveless tunic clung to her rounded belly. A grin lit her full face as she called out a welcome.

Not long now, Levi thought as they all waved back. Beckett, Laney and the baby nicknamed Muffin, since they'd declined to know the gender. A family... Levi hadn't realized how alluring that sounded until recently. Because Mara was around?

He pushed the thought away. The eager chatter of the guests relaxed him, as well as the comforting sight of Willow and Mara safely in the jeep a careful distance away. They'd caught up easily after skirting the hotel property.

Mara had the guests' luggage in the vehicle along with Willow. He had to admit her idea of a sag wagon was a good one. All Mara's ideas for the ranch seemed to be good ones. He knew she would cherry-pick all the best pictures Willow took during their inaugural tour to include on the website and in the newsletter.

Did she think she could talk him out of selling? Or force him? He didn't believe she would go so far as to legally block the sale. That was a bluff, he was pretty sure.

"Hey," Austin said, turning in the saddle, "Ground Control to Levi."

Levi blinked. "Sorry. What?"

"You getting the gate or me?"

He'd been so lost in his thoughts and the happy chatter of the guests, he hadn't realized they'd come to the entrance that led onto Gene's property. A painted sign read *Campsite ahead. Come on in and close the gate behind you.*

He hopped out of the saddle and opened the latch. His nerves prickled as they rode past Teegan and Amelia's house. The shades were drawn, and the place looked empty. Probably everyone was at the campsite. As they rode on, the shadow of the cliffs fell over them. The guests stopped to snap pictures of the rocky, silvered mountain. Again he felt a skittering of the nerves, and he turned in the saddle. Mara and Willow were still tucked safely behind them. They waved to the cop stationed along the road.

Austin picked up on his tension. "What's on your mind?"

"Nothing. Wind's picking up."

"Yeah. Best to get these folks settled in camp."

They rode to the flat area which was ringed with tents, pop-up campers and folding chairs. Away from the tents, a campfire crackled in an enormous stone circle, around which were arranged more chairs. Couples sat chatting with coffee mugs in hand. In the distance were the porta-potties Gene had promised his guests. Farther away from the fire was a table with crafts where the children clustered. Amelia sat there, helping the youngsters fill tiny bottles with different-colored sand. Peter was bent over a bottle, doing his best with a tiny funnel. Amelia raised her face to laugh at her son when she caught sight of Levi. Her gaze swept to Mara and Willow. She didn't exactly frown, but the smile definitely left her face in a hurry.

He and Austin helped the guests dismount.

"Best time ever," Mr. Johnson said, pumping Levi's hand and insisting on giving him a tip.

"Honestly. I hope we can come back and visit your stables year after year."

Levi hoped he concealed the stab of pain. "Yes, sir. We'd like that."

Eve and Doris thanked him as well before they joined the mingling visitors to find their assigned campsites. Gene's rental tents were already erected and marked with numbers.

"Clever, huh?" Jerry smiled at Levi. He was dressed the part of the Mule Team driver, complete with leather boots and dust-covered clothes. He stretched his arm as if he was working out a cramp. "I mean, the way he laid out the whole place. Got yourself quite a shiner, Levi. You're a trouble magnet."

Levi watched Mara and Willow get out of the jeep and walk toward them.

"Have you dug your trailer out?" Levi asked.

He sighed. "Well, now, not completely." He scuffed his heel in the dirt. "I feel really bad about that still. You and your girlfriend could have been seriously hurt."

Girlfriend? "She's not my girlfriend."

Jerry quirked a bristly brow. "My mistake."

He wasn't sure how to keep the conversation going, but he didn't have to. Willow and Mara caught up. Willow had her enormous camera, and Mara held a clipboard with a series of neat checks on it. "We made sure all the belongings were accounted for by our guests. I told them we'd hang on to them for a few minutes while they found their campsite."

Always efficient.

"Have you seen Teegan around?" Levi asked Jerry, casually.

"Earlier he was adding wood to the fire. Don't see him now. Might be fetching more logs. I gotta go find the little cowboys' room. See you later."

Levi noticed Amelia and Peter were gone from the craft table when he looked.

"The Johnsons are ready for their luggage," Austin said. "I'll take it over to their tent."

"You don't need to do that," Levi told his brother.

Austin grinned. "What? And miss my chance to earn a tip?" He hefted the bags with his good arm and followed the Johnsons. The sisters refused help and toted their own bags.

"That's it, then," Levi announced. "We're clear. Austin and I will take the horses back. We'll be right behind you."

But Mara wasn't listening. Her gaze was lost somewhere in the rock cliff that backed the campsite. She hadn't forgotten her mission.

Get it done and get out of here, his instincts whispered.

Fast.

* * *

Mara clutched the clipboard as she walked away from the tent area. Wisps of smoke from the campfire tickled her nostrils. She looked up at the mountains in the distance, caught in a blaze of noontime sun. All around her were people enjoying one another's company. Standing there in such an unbelievably perfect landscape, she could almost forget about all that had happened—her brother, the crash, the harsh voice in the hospital.

Why aren't you dead?

Who could be so evil as to want her dead? Or Seth? Or Corinne…

Thoughts of her sister crowded close again. Being in this place brought the memories to the surface. Somewhere in this breathtaking region, Corinne had taken her last breath.

It was probably silly, imagining some clue in the painting, but she was here, and she did not want to leave any proverbial stones unturned. She closed her eyes, trying to recreate the crudely painted cliff in the artwork she'd bought from Amelia. The teapot cloud floating over a sloppily painted mountain.

Willow had shown her the indistinct photo on her camera again, just before they'd come. The rock in the painting was split into four parts, like the fingers of a hand. It had been so familiar, and she was certain she'd seen a similar view on Gene's property. Surely there would be something in the scenery that would remind her of the painting. Light stung her eyes as she opened them and tried to see things afresh. The warm, sandy ground seemed to exert a magnetic pull.

Levi kept right next to her as she wandered away from the campsite, toward the vast acres of rock-studded plain. The vista was dazzling, but nothing stood out as she'd prayed it would. The four-fingered rock had to be there, but she saw no sign of it. Levi stopped her with a touch to her forearm.

"We should go back, Mara."

"But…" she said, ready to dig in her heels. Then she sighed. He was right, and she'd agreed to be cautious. This plain rippled into foothills, which stretched away into the vast sprawl of the mountains. They were so far away, it would have been impossible to depict any particular formation. What had she expected? This wasn't some Nancy Drew novel where the clue would be revealed and there would be a happy ending for one and all.

He grasped her hand, and she squeezed his fingers as they returned. "Thank you for letting me look," she said. "I know that wasn't strictly in our agreement."

"I wanted you to find something, too." The warmth of his hand kept her pushing through a sudden tide of exhaustion.

She didn't want her failed mission to detract from the success of the day. "Anyway, I guess we completed our first official Camp Town Days tour, so that counts for something."

"Thanks to you. You're a natural at this horse-tour business."

She laughed. "I—" Her words failed. Electricity zinged through her body. She squinted against the smoke from the campfire. Behind the flames, the pile of rocks rose into the sky, losing itself into the blue. "Look."

They moved closer to the fire, standing upwind of the crackling blaze. She pointed, and he peered after her finger. When he still could not see it, she slid her hand under his chin, avoiding hurting his bruised flesh, and gently tipped his head up.

The arch of his brows told her he'd seen it. A shelf of rock that was split into four parts... like fingers on the hand, like the painting. She reached for her cell phone to text Willow.

Something buzzed from overhead.

"What is that?" A woman sitting facing the campfire jerked around.

Levi stared up at the sky, arms out as if he could ward off whatever was coming.

"Run, Mara!" he shouted.

The thing swooped closer, diving straight at her.

FIFTEEN

She thought at first it was a bird, until it came close enough that she could see the metal propellers. A toy? But this toy was diving straight toward her, ready to plow nose first into her face. She ducked, and it sailed up but not out of sight. It hovered, circled, reoriented to try again.

"It's a drone," somebody yelled. "Who's flying it?"

She had no extra brainpower to look around as the drone was now turning and readying for another attack. Whoever was at the controls, their target was her and no one else.

"Mara," Levi called, reaching to pull her away. He stumbled over an exposed rock and went down to one knee. The drone was speeding through the air in a sizzling blur.

Fear turned to something else. The muscles in her arms acted of their own accord. The drone was so close now she could make out the blinking green light on the front. *Come and get me.*

Go ahead. She stepped away from Levi and swung the clipboard with all the strength she could summon. It cracked into the drone with a satisfying crunch, sending the machine whirling backward in an untidy arc. A propeller broke off. The drone tumbled once and dropped into the campfire.

She stood there clutching the clipboard and breathing hard. Levi was next to her now, gaping at the melting mess in the flames. She caught her breath, tucked the clipboard under her arm and gave him a shaky smile.

"Handled," she said.

His expression was a mixture of horror and appreciation. "I'll say." He immediately guided her to Willow's jeep. Somehow, she got her legs to cooperate. Willow caught up. "Austin took off to look for the drone operator."

"Most of those things only have a range of a few miles, so he or she will be close." Levi continued to hurry her past the spectators who were now crowding near the campfire to see what had happened to the drone.

Close. Her mouth went dry. As she approached the jeep, Levi opened the passenger door and ushered her inside. Willow slid into the driver's seat and started the engine. "Drive to meet the officer we passed on the way in. Tell him what happened."

He turned.

"Where are you going?" Mara asked.

"To help Austin. Don't stop, and don't get out of the car."

Be careful, she wanted to say, but he surprised her by bending and pressing a kiss to her lips.

He chuckled. "Now I remember why you always beat Seth and me at batting practice."

Her lips were still tingling as he closed the door. Willow guided the car toward the police officer. "I've seen those things used for aerial photography, and even search-and-rescue stuff lately, but never to terrorize someone. Who would do that?"

"Someone close," Mara said as she looked out the window. The four-fingered rock shadowed the vehicle as they left. It was certainly the same formation in the painted picture that had been stolen from Levi's truck.

As they rolled on she realized that Gene's ranch was the only place that offered a clear view of the rock. So whoever painted it had to have been right here on the property. They passed Teegan's house. A wave of cold prickles washed over her as she noted that his kitchen window looked right out onto that very rock, as did a side window in Gene's house.

The drone hadn't been an accident or a prank. It had been sent to zero in on her. Why? To prevent her from making the connection between the painting and the actual location?

Too late.

Now she saw the crowd beginning to scatter. Teegan appeared holding Peter, facing his wife. Had he come from his yard? Easy enough for him to have launched a drone from there. She saw Gene gripping a pair of barbecue tongs, apparently getting the story from Jerry who pointed a finger at the departing jeep. Any one of them could have slunk behind the nearest rock tumble and piloted the drone and then joined in the melee, appearing completely innocent. The remote control might even be small enough to fit in a pocket.

Mara felt as if all their eyes were locked on the jeep as they drove to the police officer. He must have gotten word that something was happening because he rolled to meet them.

"Jude's been patrolling the main road. He's approaching now," the officer said. "I'll escort you to the gate to meet him before I head to the campsite."

They nodded, rolled up their window and continued to the gate. Though she knew it had been a minor threat and the drone strike would not necessarily have inflicted a grievous wound, she was relieved when Jude's vehicle came into sight.

Still, she would only feel completely at ease

when Levi showed up at the ranch without further incident.

Back at the Rocking Horse, she and Willow settled in at the kitchen table, distracted by the attention of Banjo and the mewing cat. Jude checked in briefly, earning a bark from Banjo, until he flipped him a dog biscuit.

"Do you carry doggy treats in your pockets?" Willow said. "I didn't realize that was standard cop equipment."

"Started keeping a bag of dog chews in my vehicle after I met Banjo. I guess I should add kitty treats, too, now."

When he had ascertained they were okay and got Mara's explanation of what happened, he nodded. "I'll be on the phone for a while, so I'll step outside."

Willow fixed tea for them both. Mara cradled the mug gratefully. "So much has happened since I came to Furnace Falls it makes my head spin."

"It sure has. I, uh, misjudged you. I guess it's a good time to apologize."

"No need. I was looking down from my high horse," she said with a sigh. "I know Levi better now. I understand his motives."

Willow slid into her chair, her eyebrow raised. "You know I love my brother to distraction."

Mara stiffened, eyeing her warily.

"I thought until recently that his whole heart was in this ranch, but I'm beginning to think there's room for something else." She smiled. "Or should I say someone else."

Heat began to crawl up her neck. "Me?"

"Uh-huh."

"It's not like that between us."

"He doesn't kiss just anyone, you know."

"Well, I, um…"

She held up a palm. "Not my business, but as you know I'm protective of him so I butt in when I feel the impulse. How do you feel about Levi? Because I can tell he feels pretty strongly about you."

How did she feel? She felt as though he was the most amazing man she'd ever met: quiet, strong, loving, tenderhearted—as much as he tried to hide it. She sidestepped the question. "He's selling the ranch."

She gaped. "Why would he do that?"

"I don't think he wants it known, but he intends to give back the money Seth spent so my family can pay for therapy."

"That sounds like Levi. But that doesn't mean you two couldn't be together, does it?" She waved a hand. "I put you on the spot. I have a way of doing that. You don't have to answer. Just promise me you won't hurt my brother. He cares about you, a lot. If you don't love him, tell him flat out. He's too good and too sincere to play games."

"No games. I can assure you of that." But their arrangement was temporary. And hadn't that been the plan all along? Mara had come grudgingly, and Levi hadn't wanted her there any more than she'd desired to be there. They were together purely out of convenience.

He feels pretty strongly about you... She'd thought so, imagined something between them. Now she wasn't sure about anything. She was grateful beyond measure when she saw Austin and Levi riding onto the property, each of them leading two horses behind them. She jumped up to fix a pitcher of ice water and set out glasses, mostly to keep from talking to Willow.

The men entered, followed by Jude.

"No sign of the controller," Levi said.

Austin drank deeply. "I figure he was hiding around the side of the rock pile, maybe. After Mara took out the drone, he must have joined in the group as if nothing happened."

Jude smiled. "Mara, I'm thinking of including your drone-handling technique in our police training, in case we should ever need it."

Mara laughed. "My brother always says swing for the bleachers." Thinking about how Seth would laugh sent a wave of sorrow washing over her.

"Unfortunately, the machine is incinerated, so no prints there. Drones weighing more than 8.8 grams are supposed to be registered with the FAA and visibly labeled with the number. If there was one, it's unreadable, but we'll have the techs examine it, anyway."

"Teegan's house looks right out on the four-fingered rock," Mara said. She explained her theory of the painting. "The drone could be his way of discouraging me from making that connection."

"It's sketchy," Jude said. "There's no proof that your sister painted it. Nothing to tie Teegan to any of the attacks on you. Nothing to justify a search warrant."

Mara deflated.

"So another attack on Mara, and there's not a thing we can do?" Levi's hands were balled into fists on the table.

"We'll look closer at the drone. We're still processing the scene at J and K. That's all I can give you for now." He rose and tossed another dog cookie to Banjo. "Don't get up, boy. I'm on my way out."

Willow and Austin left together shortly thereafter.

Mara felt suddenly claustrophobic. "I'm going to visit the horses."

He didn't answer, just got up and walked to

the fence alongside her. She wanted to be alone, to sort out in her mind the drone attack and Willow's probing comments. Why should they impact her so? Because Willow knew Levi better than anyone on the planet, and she believed he might just be developing serious feelings for Mara.

They stood side by side, elbows propped on the warped fence rails. "Levi…" she started.

He looked at her, silent, waiting patiently for her to continue. Her heart stirred at the quiet blue gaze, and electricity tingled in the spot where her shoulder touched his. And then words failed her.

He cocked his head for a moment, and then he turned slowly. His lips were only inches away. Was Willow right? Was it love he was beginning to feel for Mara? And what was the answering echo inside her own heart?

He drew her close and pressed a kiss to her cheek, then her temple. What was this feeling that burgeoned between them? Did he feel as confused as she did? They were recent antagonists, he was her brother's best friend, her life was not here in Furnace Falls, and maybe his wasn't either if he sold the Rocking Horse. He was quiet, laid-back, content, and she was none of those things. But she could not escape the feeling that God had brought her here, right here, for a reason.

She heard the steady beat of his heart as she laid her head on his chest. It was such a sense of comfort that she almost didn't hear the approaching car.

Levi immediately let go of Mara and stepped in front of her as the unfamiliar sedan rolled up the drive. He wished he had his rifle.

"It's my dad." Mara broke around him and started to run toward the vehicle. She was gasping, trembling, and he caught up with her as the car stopped.

Mr. Castillo got out. Levi searched his face looking for signs of what he most feared.

Mara stopped short of her father, hands pressed to her mouth, face pale as moonlight. "Oh, Daddy. It's not Seth. He's not…"

Her father's brows creased. "No, no, honey. I'm sorry. I didn't think how you'd react. Seth is okay."

Mara sobbed, and Levi longed to comfort her, but it was not his place. Mr. Castillo wrapped her in a hug and rocked her from side to side until she could regain some composure.

"I thought, when I saw you there…" she said, rubbing the tears from her cheeks as he let her go.

"I wanted to talk to you face to face." He took in the surroundings. Levi grimaced as he imagined what Mr. Castillo would think about the ramshackle cabin where his daughter was staying, the barking of Banjo who had mercifully been shut in the kitchen.

"Let me secure the dog, and you two can talk in the house." Levi hurried off and ushered Banjo and Tiny into the back room with a handful of treats as a lure. There was only enough time to straighten the chairs and pick up one of Banjo's discarded chew bones before Mara and her father came in.

Mara looked calmer, he thought, but with a touch of wariness.

"I'll leave you to chat," Levi said.

"Stay," Mr. Castillo said. "This concerns you, too."

Now he felt plenty wary himself. Mr. Castillo declined his offer of instant coffee. "First off, good news. The doctors are discussing Seth's discharge."

Mara gasped, and he could not restrain a whoop of pleasure.

"That's the best news I could have gotten," Mara said, after a gulp.

Her father held up a palm. "They're recommending a rehab facility. We've decided to take him back home to Henderson since there's one close to our home."

Levi nodded. What had he expected? "Do you know when, sir?"

"Not yet. Seth's confusion is clearing up, and he's been talking incessantly about this ranch. I'm going to have to break it to him that he's not coming back here."

"Dad," Mara said, "are you saying he's not going to recover?"

Her father sighed. "No, of course not, but he can't pick up and resume his dream of running this place for who-knows-how-long. I'm not sure he'll ever accept it."

Levi knew it was time to make it all real. "He will…if you tell him I'm selling."

Mr. Castillo's eyes flew wide. "What?"

"I'm selling it, and I'll return Seth's half of the payment. There won't be a ranch to go back to for Seth." The words felt like glass shards as they cut their way out of his mouth.

Mr. Castillo was silent when Mara jumped in.

"I don't want him to, Dad. I won't give legal permission on Seth's behalf."

Mr. Castillo heaved a sigh. "Honey, I know it's not what anyone wanted, but we have to be realistic." He turned to Levi. "I appreciate what you're doing. I know you love this ranch, and this is a sacrifice."

Levi didn't dare speak.

Mr. Castillo stopped Mara's next comment.

"Now. I want you to tell me what exactly is going on here. I overheard Jude Duke talking on his phone while he was at the hospital asking some follow-up questions. I want to know what's happening and what this has to do with your sister."

Mara looked at him with rounded eyes. There was no choice now but to tell him everything.

By the end of the story, his expression had gone stark. He looked from Mara to Levi and back to his daughter. "Listen to me, both of you. I don't understand what's going on with these messages and the attacks. I would love nothing more than to believe my baby…" His voice broke and he swallowed. "To believe that Corinne was alive. All this time…all these years not knowing if she ran off to live somewhere else or someone murdered her. It's so tantalizing to think there is an answer, but Mara, I cannot and will not allow you to risk yourself to find out anything more. We'll hire a private detective, just like we did when she first ran away. It will have to wait until we have the funds, after we get your brother settled."

"But Dad," Mara said softly, "by that time there might be nothing to find."

"So be it," he said harshly. "We've lost Corinne. We almost lost Seth. Your mother and I cannot endure any more."

She reached across the table and took his hand. "I'm sorry, Dad."

"Don't be sorry. Say you'll come home with us to Henderson."

"I'm… I'm helping here. I promised…"

"No need," Levi said. Somehow he forced himself to say it. "The ranch is done. I can handle the remaining tasks until it's sold. It's time for you to go home."

Oh, the hurt that spiraled through those ink-dark eyes. He knew he'd cut her to the quick, made her feel like a work assistant whose contract had come to an end. A jerk, that's what he was, and a liar, but he could think of no other way to restore what was left of the Castillo family. With every muscle screaming in protest, he stood.

"Mr. Castillo, thank you for coming. I will continue to pray with everything in me that Seth recovers, and you'll have his money back as soon as I can get it to you." And then he walked out, onto the sunlit ranch that would soon be taken from him, away from the woman who'd changed him from the inside out.

SIXTEEN

Mara could hear the parade as it passed noisily through town on Wednesday morning. This time she had not bothered to pressure Levi to let her go. He'd pressed his siblings to help, she was sure, to lead the visitors through the parade and back to the property on Gene's campsite. Jude was sitting on the porch, alternately speaking into his radio and eyeing the shenanigans of Banjo and Tiny. He was her babysitter, pure and simple. His life would also be easier after she did what Levi and her father had asked and left Furnace Falls. Sorrow made her weary and flat as she packed up her belongings.

It's time for you to go home.

The words were benign, but they cut her so deep that she could not help but admit that her feelings for Levi were profound. Dare she recognize that she was beginning to love the man? The same man who had just told her to leave and not look back. There was a sense that something had torn inside her, something that would not ever be mended.

Her father called to tell her that Seth would be released to rehab on Friday. She intended to drive ahead of them to Henderson, once she retrieved Seth's SUV from the repair shop the next day. So what was she supposed to do in the meantime? It was awkward and painful to be hanging out on the Rocking Horse with Levi.

After the parade, he returned with the horses and let them into the pasture. He'd begun to rub them down, when she let herself through the gate. "I'll do that."

He jerked a look at her. "Not necessary."

"I need to do something," she said.

"Mara..." He blew out a breath and closed his mouth.

She couldn't help herself. She faced him, gripping the curry brush like a shield. "I know you're bent on doing right by my family, but do you really want me to leave?" Why had she said it? Now she sounded like some sort of desperate high schooler. Perhaps like Corinne had come across in her phone messages and texts to Teegan?

He reached out but stopped short of touching her. The silence stretched between them. "It doesn't matter what I want."

Her soul surged.

"But you need to go. There's nothing here for you," he continued.

Nothing. He turned away and trudged out of the pasture and started to talk to Jude. *Maybe he was telling his cousin his babysitting duties would be over soon*, she thought bitterly.

Rubbing angrily at a tear that coursed down her cheek, she set to work, removing the saddles and bridles from the horses. Brushing them down soothed her and the animals.

She was mulling over how to stay far away from Levi and pass the long hours until she could pick up the car, when a truck with J and K Excavation on the side jerked to a halt in front of the house. Jerry got out. She took one look at what he had in his hand and ran out to meet him as he interrupted Jude and Levi's conversation.

There could be no mistaking the dirty bent green notebook he was waving around. "Look here what I found."

Jude took it from his hand. "Your old appointment book?"

"Uh-huh. Took a lot of digging, I'll tell you, but I figured it was the least I could do since you almost got buried in there, Mara."

Her pulse hammered. "Find October twenty-eighth, the day I got the message from your phone. What does it say? Where was Jerry then?"

Jude flipped a few pages and read the date. He frowned. "Teegan's place, bidding on a job for his patio."

Finally. Tangible evidence.

"That must have been where I lost my phone. But I still can't figure out who made that call to you." Jerry rubbed a hand over his bald head.

Mara watched Jude's face. Was it enough to convince him?

"Thanks, Jerry," Jude said. "I'll keep this, okay?"

"Sure," Jerry said, climbing back into his truck. "I really wish I still had the cell phone. Those things are expensive."

They watched him drive away.

"Jude," she said slowly. "The picture, and the messages and now this appointment book. It all leads back to the Warrington property. Is it enough now to get a search warrant?"

"Still sketchy, but I'll see what I can do."

"Mara, your father wants—" Levi started.

"You don't have to tell me what my father wants, Levi," she snapped. "Don't worry. This is a police matter and I'm leaving tomorrow, as planned. Okay?"

He didn't answer, and she whirled away, hurrying back to the horses.

Her father's tortured face surfaced in her memory. She knew he'd insisted the whole thing be dropped, but Jude's search could answer the question that had plagued her since she got that strange text message... *Marbles*.

What had really happened to Corinne?

Levi finally started digging holes. He told himself it would be good to replace the two wobbly fence posts, but really it was to keep him from beelining straight for Mara's door and telling her he didn't really want her to leave.

But it was what was best for Mara. Safest. That's what love was, wanting the best for someone else more than your own desires.

Love? The thought hit him so powerfully that he dropped the shovel. Retrieving it, he chided himself. Not love. Concern. Honor. Fondness for his best friend's sister. Respect. Not love. There was no point in even thinking of it. Whatever they'd felt was over now that she was leaving and he was selling.

He wiped the sweat from his face and kept digging until the new holes were significantly deeper than they should have been. For the umpteenth time he checked his watch. Jude had been gone for two hours. He was probably knee-deep in executing the search warrant.

His restless energy would not subside. The cabin seemed to call to him. Should he go offer Mara something? Water or a snack? He didn't dare, coward that he was. It was simply too painful to see the wounded look on her face. But she'd never even wanted to come to Furnace Falls in the first place. The whole situation was maddening.

He drank two glasses of iced tea, and he sat morosely on the couch trying to ignore his laptop. There was no putting it off. He'd seen the email from the potential buyer earlier in the day, but he hadn't wanted to open it. Finally he did.

Levi, on Google Earth it indicates the property encompasses a creek. Intermittent or perennial?

Fancy words, he thought. He typed in response Intermittent. It was Death Valley, after all, he thought grumpily. A body of water was hardly going to stick around through the warm weather months when it hit a hundred and thirty degrees. A wave of sorrow washed over him. Soon this piece of earth would not be his, anyway. Idly, he opened the Google Earth app and put in the address for the Rocking Horse. From far away it was a vague, indistinct patch of brown until he zoomed closer.

He saw the dried creek bed, the furrowed ground where his horses were free to roam as they pleased. The clustered pines under which he'd first spotted Banjo, starved and injured. The places that were straight-up blessings in his mind would mean nothing at all to a stranger.

Swallowing down the sadness, he tried to distract himself by switching locations to Gene's property. If he zoomed enough, he could make out the strange four-fingered rock formation. No matter how things turned out, he'd always think of Mara when he imagined that big pile of rock. Would she be leaving with answers about Corinne or more questions?

He was about to click off, when something caught his eye. He leaned closer, zoomed in even more. What did it mean, really, that strange shape on his screen? His blood went icy. He zoomed in and out and in again to make sure it wasn't some sort of optical illusion. Was he witnessing an answer to the riddle or the truth that would crush the Castillo family? He didn't want to tell Mara, but the burning in his gut would not be ignored.

Lord, please help me not to hurt her anymore, he prayed before he tucked the laptop under his arm and hurried to her cabin.

Mara stared at the laptop while Levi drove. He'd not been able to reach Jude on his cell phone.

"We'll find the nearest cop on the property and explain it," Levi had said.

She peered again at the faint image that would only be visible from above. The bird's-eye view revealed a rectangular outline where the shrubbery was a different hue, parched and deadened while the grass around it showed a dusky green. The rectangle was about a hundred feet from Teegan's backyard, obscured behind haphazard clusters of rock and tall grasses. His window looked right out on the place.

"It's something underground," Levi had said.

Something. Like a bomb shelter or a subterranean storage room, completely concealed except the outline.

It might mean nothing at all.

Or it might mean everything.

One way or another, Jude had to include it in the search. Mara tried to unclench her jaw and breathe deeply. It could be a simple storage area, nothing more innocuous than that. But her instincts would simply not stop screaming. *Find out. Now.*

Levi pulled through the gate into chaos. Horses were running in every direction with their owners trying to catch them. A mare neatly avoided their vehicle by wheeling around and galloping off.

Levi rolled down his window. "What's going on?"

Jerry jogged up and cast him a quick look.

"Someone unhitched the horses and scared 'em with a firecracker. Trying to get 'em all under control again."

No accident this time, she thought.

"Have you seen Jude?" Levi said.

"Parked at Teegan's, I think."

"What are the chances someone startled the horses at the same time Jude is serving his search warrant?" Levi's tone was grim.

She did not answer, jaw tight.

Levi eased through the scrambling people and horses and increased speed until they rolled up to Teegan's driveway. There were two police cars there. One officer was trying to assist in rounding up the horses. Jude appeared in the doorway, his hands in latex gloves.

Levi and Mara hurried to show him the aerial photo. He stared at it and then let out a gusty exhale. "All right. I'll start there."

"I want to see," Mara said.

Levi and Jude both went silent.

"That's not really a good idea," Jude said.

"I'll take you back to the ranch," Levi said. "Jude will call as soon as he knows anything."

Mara realized her hands were balled into fists. "I understand that you might be about to find out something terrible down in there. Or maybe you'll find nothing but lawn mowers and jelly jars. I'm not asking to go with you or mess up a police investigation, but I want to stay here until you know for sure this isn't about my sister." Her eyes burned, and she felt as if she was igniting from the inside out.

Jude shifted. "No, Mara. I'm sorry."

"I am not going unless you have me arrested." She flung down the gauntlet, heedless of the consequences. The only thing that mattered now was the truth about Corinne, however tragic it might be. "This is my last day in Furnace Falls, and I'm going to stay here until the search is done. Period."

After a moment, Jude sighed. "Wait in Levi's truck. Do not get out of that vehicle. Are we clear?"

She nodded.

"Have you found anything in Teegan's house yet?" Levi asked.

"Haven't finished." His expression darkened. "I should tell you it looks like they're gone."

"Gone?" Mara said. "Teegan and Amelia?"

"And Peter. Their luggage is missing, as though they left in a hurry."

A block of ice settled in her stomach. "They wouldn't have run, not now in the middle of Camp Town Days, unless they'd done something bad."

Levi considered. "Think they excited the horses to create a distraction?"

"I am not going to speculate. I have an officer trying to track down Gene at the campsite. Maybe he can shed some light. Wait in the truck," Jude said quietly. "Please."

Levi led her back to the truck, and she climbed inside, mentally fogged.

Levi held out his hand to her, and she took it.

"Levi," she finally managed, "do you think my sister…?" Her nightmares took hold of her. *Died down in that bunker? Was kept a prisoner all these years?* She couldn't force herself to say anymore.

"We'll know soon." He quietly began to pray. Though she could not make any sound, her heart followed with yearning.

God, no matter how it goes, let me hear the truth, and give me the strength to survive it.

SEVENTEEN

It was the longest hour Levi could remember, longer even than when he'd been forced into a wreck in Mara's car and hung upside down until help arrived. The answer to the strange attacks on him, Seth and Mara was finally going to be unearthed. He was certain of it. He was equally certain it would be useless to try to convince Mara to wait back at the Rocking Horse. She sat next to him, silent as midnight, fingers twined tightly in his. At least she would allow him to offer her what little he could now. He quivered inside to think about what she might find out in a matter of moments.

But most likely it was nothing, right? The underground structure could be innocent.

A squad car barreled into the property, red lights strobing, followed by another.

Why so many police cars if it was nothing?

Mara's grip tightened. In the distance, they could make out flashlights slicing through the gloom of the approaching sunset. Her breathing had gone shallow as the minutes ticked by and no news came. A half hour limped past. He was about to try one more time to take her back to the ranch, when his phone buzzed. He put it on speaker.

"It's Jude," he said. "Can you bring Mara here?"

"What did you find?" she cried.

"I need you to be strong now, Mara. Levi's going to escort you over here along with my officer. It will be over soon. Promise."

Over soon.

Levi helped her out of the car. "We'll just take it slow," he said, noting her legs were trembling. She clung to Levi, and they made their way over to the light the police must have put up.

When they were almost there, she stopped. "I feel dizzy."

He held on to her, chafing her arms. "It's okay. You don't have to do anything you don't want to."

"I have to see." But would she be able to withstand the sight that would meet her eyes soon enough? All he could do was offer his own strength to bolster hers. He thought of his own siblings—Willow, Austin—his cousins. What would they find in that bunker? Would it destroy Mara? Her parents?

Her phone buzzed, and she checked the screen. "It's my dad." She sucked in a breath. "I can't tell him. Not until we know."

They reached a small wooden door, lying almost flat to the ground. It was obscured by a layer of grass, bisected only at the borders where it had been lifted open.

Levi turned to look back at the houses. Mara followed his gaze. Gene's house did not have any windows facing the underground shelter, but Teegan would have a view from his upstairs. *What did you do, Teegan?*

Jude stopped her. "You can't go in. We've got to photograph and dust for prints and collect fibers. I'm going to allow you to look, all right? Just look."

But she didn't move, frozen to the spot.

Levi just held her hand and stood silent and steady. After a few moments, she nodded. "Okay." It came out in a whisper.

They walked to the edge and looked down.

At first she could not process what she was seeing. There was a room illuminated by an electric lamp that hung from a cement ceiling. It was tiny, no more than ten feet by ten feet, with no windows. Inside was a twin bed, the covers tumbled and twisted. There was a commode and a plastic water pitcher on the only table. A shallow shelf next to the bed held several paperback books. There was no one inside.

"I don't understand," Mara said. "Was she… was there someone here?"

"Long dark hairs on the pillow case."

Long dark hairs. She fingered her own strands, dark. Her mouth went dry.

Jude beamed his penlight at the door that covered the opening. "There was a tiny piece of paper jammed inside the lock which kept it from fastening properly. We think whoever was in here escaped, recently."

The shock shuddered through her body, and she would have collapsed if Levi hadn't held her up. "My sister? She's alive, then. Where did she go? Where could she run? Do you think Teegan took her?"

"If indeed the person was your sister, and that's a big if, Mara—" Jude started.

"Teegan might have caught her running," Levi said. "Realized he couldn't cover it up anymore and made her go with them."

"Possible. A K-9 team is coming to search the property. We have roadblocks set up and a BOLO. Got cops at the airport. They won't get far."

"And Gene?"

But she already knew. "He won't say anything to incriminate his son. He'd lie, conceal evidence, whatever, wouldn't he?" The injustice of it choked her. He would protect his son, yet allow him to imprison someone else's child.

"If he knows something, we'll hold on to him. Matter of time before we find him, too."

Jude eased them back away from the opening. "There's nothing now for you two to do here. Go back to the ranch, and I will call you with updates."

Mara stared into the small prison. Had it been Corinne's cage for nearly five years? And where was she now? She felt as if the stars were going to swallow her up as Levi took her back to his vehicle. The police were questioning the campers, now that the horses were under control. They drove in complete silence back to the Rocking Horse.

She wanted to cry, to wail. As she got out of the truck, Banjo and Tiny ran over to sniff her. Banjo whined, as if he could sense her torture. "It isn't fair," she said. "Where is she? Was that even her in that bunker?"

Levi shook his head. "I wish I could answer that." He took her in his arms and held her close. "All I can say is that I'll be right here for you, no matter how it turns out."

Right here? On a ranch that would soon be sold? After he'd told her to go home with her parents? It was too much to process, too much to endure. His arm stayed tight around her shoulders as he led her to the cabin and opened the door for her.

"Are you sure you don't want to stay in the main house? You can have my bed, and I will sleep on the sofa."

"No, thank you," she mumbled, head spinning. "I'm going to try and lie down for a while and clear my head." Banjo and Tiny followed her in. She closed the door and rested her forehead against the old wood.

Corinne, where are you?

She sank fully clothed on the bed and sobbed. Sleep. She craved the escape from the tumult. At long last, eyes closed, prayers exhausted, empty of tears, she dozed.

Until her phone rang. The police, she thought in terror. What had they found? Could she endure it?

"Hello?" she said, heart in her throat.

"Marbles."

Levi didn't bother to try and sleep. He'd paced until he was tired and then slumped on the sofa. He dozed for what seemed like a moment, when he heard something on the front porch. Instantly, he was wide awake, reaching for his rifle. He eased the curtain back just far enough to make out a silhouette of someone holding an oil lamp, one of those old kinds they used for the reen-actments. The flame illuminated a flash of arm, no more.

He tiptoed to the door, one hand on the knob, the other on his rifle, and gave himself a slow count of three.

One.

He thought he heard the murmur of voices. Were there two people?

Two.

He squeezed the rifle in his hand and yanked the door wide.

Whoever it was screamed and dropped a cell phone.

"Stay right there," he shouted. Mara's cabin door flung open, and she plunged into the court-yard. She would run right into the intruder.

"Mara, stop."

It was as if she hadn't heard him. "No!" she shouted. Running, she stumbled to a knee, righted herself and kept on going until she skid-ded to a halt at the porch step. Banjo followed her, barking fit to burst.

He saw now it was a woman on the porch, ex-tremely thin, long hair wild in the lantern light. Her fingers clutched the lantern in a death grip. The dark eyes were unmistakable, so like her sister's.

"Corinne?" Mara whispered.

After a few starts and stops, the woman spoke. Her voice was hoarse and raspy. "I came to find you. I kept a phone that I found in the house. I sent you a text."

"Yes," Mara whispered. "I got it."

She chewed her lip, face slack. "I tried to send more but service in the bunker was spotty, and then the phone went dead. I found a phone charger when I escaped. I heard him say you were coming to the Rocking Horse with Seth. I thought you would be here, at the ranch." Banjo started barking, and she jerked in fright.

Levi quieted the dog.

"Who said that?" Mara asked, gently. "Teegan?"

"No," came a voice from the darkness. "Put down the rifle, Levi."

Gene stepped into the light. He was holding a revolver.

Levi did not lower his rifle. "What's going on, Gene?"

Gene spoke genially as if he was shooting the breeze. "Just came for her. Come here, Corinne. I've been thinking this would happen since the moment Jerry's phone went missing. He dropped it, the dope, while he was on our property. I brought it into the kitchen, but you found it first, didn't you?" He shook his head at Corinne as if she was an errant child. "Sent your sister a message? Jerry told me he got a call from Mara that she was coming to town." He actually chuckled. "You hid that phone well, because I tore that bunker apart many times, and I never found it. Sneaky girl. Phones and postcards and texts, oh my." His soft chuckled made the hair on Levi's arms stand up.

Mara grabbed Corinne's wrist. "You and your son are not going to hurt her anymore." In spite of Levi's commands, Banjo's barking reached terrific levels. The scruff of his neck was raised.

Gene stared for a moment. His voice remained calm. "Drop the rifle, quiet the dog, or I start shooting."

Mara's face blazed. "You're bluffing."

Gene's mouth tightened. "You think so? I wasn't bluffing when I shot into your brother's windshield." His tone had gone hard and dead as petrified wood. "You should have died in the hospital, like I said. None of this would have happened, then."

Levi tried to edge closer, between the women and the man who was a stranger to him now.

Mara stepped back but did not let go of her sister. "That was you?"

"We're not going to have an extended discussion here," Gene said. "Drop the rifle, Levi."

Levi stayed put. He knew if he laid the gun down, their leverage was gone. Gene fired a round at Banjo. The shot nearly deafened them. Corinne screamed. The dog tumbled over backward with a yelp. Tiny mewled and squeezed under the porch.

"Stop!" Levi hollered.

Mara clung to her sister's arm.

Gene readied another round. "Next one's for Mara."

Hot with rage, Levi put down the rifle. "Let's talk this out," he tried. "No need for anyone to get hurt."

Corinne was trembling as though she could hardly stand. Her eyes were dull and staring.

"Right." Gene tossed Mara a roll of tape. "Tape his hands behind his back."

"I won't."

"Then, I'll shoot him right now."

With a whimper, Mara used the duct tape and circled it around Levi's wrists. He flexed as much as he could. Gene took the tape and did the same with Mara. He shoved them through the front door of the house and pushed them both toward the bathroom. He took their phones. "Inside."

They stumbled in.

"My sister!" Mara screamed. "What are you going to do to her?"

He slammed the door. They heard a chair being wedged under the handle.

"Corinne!" Mara screamed.

There was a crash of glass. All Levi's nerves fired at once as the smell of burning oil trickled under the door. Gene had smashed the lantern on the floor. In a matter of moments, his house would be on fire. He set to work quickly working the tape to loosen it.

Mara was looking up at the small window. When he freed himself, he quickly ripped the tape from her wrists. He aimed several vicious kicks at the door, but it was wedged tight.

"Window is the only option. You'll fit."

"I can't leave without you."

"Oh, yes, you can."

"No," she said, grabbing at his arms.

"Mara, you have to get out or Corinne will die. They will kill her to protect themselves."

She blinked, her face a ghastly white.

Before she could offer a retort, he linked his hands together and hoisted her up. She wrenched the window open. "I'll come back for you," she called as she wriggled through.

"No. Call Jude. I'll make it out. Get away. This place is a tinderbox."

When she was gone, he exhaled. Hopefully Gene had fled and would not be a further threat to Mara. Jude would track him down, save Corinne. He tried kicking the door several more times without success. Smoke was oozing through the gap between the door and floor now, and he wet the bathroom towels and shoved them in.

He considered the tiny bathroom. The towel bar caught his attention. Strength wasn't going to get him out, but brains might.

He yanked the bar from the wall and shoved the end under the door hinge. With a huge effort, he levered the pin out of the slot. He was working on the second one when the door was wrenched open.

Mara's face was blackened, the whites of her eyes luminous in the smoky air. "Come on," she yelled.

"I told you not to come back," he snapped as he followed her.

"Since when do I follow directives?"

They stumbled free. He grabbed his fallen rifle as he searched frantically. "Where's Banjo?"

"I don't know," she said helplessly.

Jude's car roared up. "Fire department is following."

"Gene's taken Corinne," Mara panted.

Jude's eyes widened. "I didn't see them on the way in."

"They must have gone the back road off the ranch. Follow me." Levi was running toward his brother's truck. Mara leaped in while he was cranking it to life. He didn't try to argue that she should stay behind. Time was of the essence. He gunned the engine and hit the gas, speeding them past the startled horses in the near pasture.

He pushed the truck so fast they bounced and rattled over every rock and dip.

"There," Mara yelled, pointing to a turn in the road ahead. "There's his SUV."

"We can't get to the main road before him," Levi yelled back. "There's only one way to stop him, but this might not go well." He shot a look at her. "Do you trust me?"

Mara did not hesitate. "I trust you with my life."

The words fueled him, stripped away all the doubts and fears. This woman trusted him with her life and her sister's...and he loved her with everything he possessed. He took one moment to squeeze her hand and make sure her seat belt was buckled. "Hold on."

EIGHTEEN

Mara clung to the armrest as Levi shot off the road and across a bumpy pasture. They were moving so fast everything was a blur. Gene's headlights in the distance shone closer as he turned into the final bend in the road. Impossibly far away it felt. She found herself straining forward as if to hurry them along.

Corinne. Her mind could not process what she'd seen. Her sister, standing there, alive after five long years. What had happened to her? Was it Gene? Teegan? Both of them? Levi's jaw was tight, fingers gripping the wheel.

"Gonna get bumpy here."

She held on with one hand, the other braced against the dash. They dipped into a lower area that took them rocketing over uneven ruts, what had been a creek in the wet season. With anyone else she would have assumed the vehicle would not survive the terrain or they would flip at any moment, but she trusted that Levi knew every dip and swell of his land.

She trusted him.

Breath held, she tried to fight off the dizziness. Ahead, Gene's headlights plowed through the dusk, indicating he was also traveling at a high rate of speed. From somewhere she heard sirens. Jude was following, but not fast enough. He would have summoned backup, but by the time they arrived, Gene would have made it off the property.

Could this really be happening? Was it all a torturous nightmare? They hit a bump hard, and she would have smashed her head into the roof if she hadn't been braced so tightly.

Gene's headlights and Levi's tangled together in a direct intercept course.

Please, Lord, please.

If Gene made it to the main road, he could get away, escape down any number of side trails, hide long enough to kill Corinne if that's what he intended to do. Why? Teegan and Amelia would be captured. It was not necessary to kill Corinne to keep her from testifying against his son, was it?

There was no more time to think as the truck closed in on the SUV.

"He's not slowing," Levi shouted over the roar

of the engine. "I'm afraid if I try to stop them, Corinne will be hurt."

Her reply was instant. "Levi, you have to. We're her only chance." *And I trust you.* She completely, thoroughly trusted this man above all others. He could save her sister, if anyone could. He would sacrifice himself, his ranch, his future for her family, for her.

The knowledge lit her heart from the inside.

He didn't answer, just floored the accelerator. The truck jumped forward the crucial few feet, enough to plunge into the road a few yards ahead of Gene's oncoming SUV. He slammed the brake, and the truck skidded to a halt.

"Hold on!" Levi yelled.

Seconds later the SUV plowed into them from behind. A screech of metal deafened her. The impact crumpled the back of Levi's truck, hurling them forward. Levi threw an arm protectively in front of Mara. The seat belt did its job, tethering her in place with a violent jerk.

The breath was driven out of her. By the time she'd assimilated the facts…they were stopped, the SUV wedged behind them, Levi was already out of the car and running, snagging his rifle on the way. She threw open the passenger door and tumbled free.

Gene's driver door was open, the white airbags deployed. He staggered out and went to one knee, reaching for the gun in his waistband.

"Stop right there, Gene," Levi said, sighting down the barrel of his rifle. "I don't want to shoot you, but I will if you give me reason."

A trickle of blood leaked from Gene's mouth. He got to his feet, looked from Levi to Jude's police vehicle approaching in the distance. Savagely he tossed the gun to the ground and lifted his hands.

He looked hard at Mara and shook his head. "Why didn't you leave it alone?" he whispered. "Everything was perfect."

She ignored him, rushing to the passenger side. It was dented, and she tugged with all her might until it gave. As the billowed airbag subsided, she held her breath. "Corinne?" she whispered.

Inch by inch the fabric melted away, and her sister, eyes both terrified and vacant, stared at her.

Slowly, ever so slowly, Mara reached out and touched Corinne on the arm. "Hey, sis," she whispered through the clog in her throat. "It's Marbles. Everything is going to be okay now. I'm here."

Corinne didn't say a word, but tears began to stream down her face.

Her sister was alive. And Mara knew her deepest prayer had been answered at long last.

Her own tears fell as she stood by Corinne and waited for the ambulance to arrive.

Levi sat with Mara while the doctors examined Corinne. He had no idea what to say so he did things: brought coffee which she didn't drink, talked to the Castillos on the phone and tried to communicate what he understood, which wasn't much.

He sat next to her in the waiting room, holding her hand while her parents drove from Las Vegas. His brother and sister had been filled in and were presently seeing to the horses and looking for any sign of Banjo, Tiny and Rabbit. Then he subsided into silence. He had no clue if his presence provided comfort or not, but he simply could not be apart from Mara, not then, not after what she'd just gone through.

When the Castillos arrived, he got up to leave, but Mara caught his sleeve. "Please stay, Levi. Please."

And in that moment she could have asked him for the keys to Buckingham Palace and he would have done his best to get them for her. It was not the time to explore the feelings sheeting through him like sand in a windstorm. He stood by her side, quiet and still, while the Castillos tried to process what had happened.

The doctor came out to meet them. "She's underweight and mentally traumatized, but otherwise healthy. There are no signs that she was physically abused."

Her father let out a groan and closed his eyes for a moment.

"She's sedated right now, but you can sit with her. A therapist will start working with her when she wakes up." He smiled kindly. "It will be a long road, but it looks like she has a strong family around her. That's what she'll need to recover."

Jude arrived and spoke to them all before Mr. and Mrs. Castillo went into Corrine's room to sit by her side. Jude raised an eyebrow at Levi.

"Dunno how you intercepted Gene so quickly. I almost lost my transmission making it over that pasture."

Levi raised a shoulder. "I know the land."

"Yes, you do. I had a very quick conversation with Corinne in the ambulance. She says Gene was her captor. Teegan had nothing to do with it as far as she knows."

Levi pulled in a quick breath. "She was locked in a box. She might not have realized that Teegan was involved." Mara clutched his hand so tight his fingers went numb.

"It's possible she's confused, fuzzy about the facts, but she says Gene kept her locked up. There's a tunnel—we just uncovered it—that leads from the bunker to Gene's place. Every once in a while, he'd let her into the main house. One time Gene fell asleep, and she used paints to create the landscape and tucked it in Amelia's box of prints that was left around. But as she'd been about to try to get out of the house, Gene caught her and was more careful from then on. Jerry accidentally dropped his phone when he did the bid on the property. Gene intended to return it but had left it in the kitchen, and Corinne was able to steal the phone and send you a quick text. She hid it in a hole she dug in the dirt floor behind the bed. Gene looked, but he never could find it. The problem was she had no way to charge it."

"That's why I only got the one text," Mara said.

Jude nodded. "Gene said she'd confessed to him that she'd sent you a postcard before about four months ago, stuck it in their outgoing mail when he was distracted by Camp Town Days planning. When he saw your car in town that Seth brought for you to fix, he didn't realize Levi was driving, so he arranged the accident. He panicked when he heard you were coming to Furnace Falls again to see the ranch. Jerry told him you wanted to talk to him about a strange message you'd received. He tried again, hence the shooting which hospitalized Seth. Not to mention the backhoe pileup at the J and K, the jack under the saddle, the drone, et cetera. All signs point to Gene."

"Not Teegan?" Mara shook her head. "So Gene imprisoned Corinne and arranged her shoe to be found in the park to make it look like a suicide? Why? Why would he do that?"

"We're going to find out, but Gene isn't cooperating anymore, and he's lawyered up. That's why I need your help. My officers stopped Teegan, Amelia and Peter on their way to the airport. We're holding him. Amelia was allowed to take Peter home, but we've got an officer guarding her since we don't know if she was involved."

"What did Teegan tell you?" Mr. Castillo demanded. "Did he admit to any part in my daughter's imprisonment?"

Jude winced. "Remember this all has to be checked out, but what he said surprised us. From what we can gather, after you moved to Henderson, she hopped a bus to meet Teegan."

"Probably while she said she was with a friend," Mara said. "She did that all the time."

He cleared his throat. "Well, this particular time, Corinne called and called but he didn't answer. Um, this might be uncomfortable for you… Teegan says she told him during their last call that she was pregnant."

"Pregnant?" Mara gasped. Mrs. Castillo pressed trembling fingers to her mouth.

"They'd, uh, apparently been together before."

Mara groaned. "That weekend she went missing for two days. When she came home, my parents grounded her for three weeks, but she still wouldn't tell where she'd been. He must have been unfaithful to Amelia. They were together at that time."

"He never disclosed that detail to the police when we were investigating her disappearance," Jude said. "Teegan says when she called to tell him that last time, he accused her of lying, told her to get lost, that he wanted nothing to do with the child—and this is where the story unravels. Teegan claims his father told him Corinne showed up one day when he wasn't home six months after their final phone conversation. He won't say anymore, and Gene isn't talking."

"Maybe they are both lying," Levi said. "Teegan's word can't be trusted, if he'd cheat on Amelia and lie to the police about being with Corinne."

"Was there a baby? What happened to it?" Mrs. Castillo asked.

"Like I said, Teegan clammed up." Jude leaned back in his seat.

Mara took on a contemplative look. "If they are as pure and innocent as the driven snow, why did they run for the airport?" she demanded.

Levi had been thinking exactly the same thing.

"Teegan isn't talking to us," Jude said. He paused and looked at Mara. "He said he needs to speak to you."

"Me?"

"You don't have to," Levi said. "The guy is dirty, no matter what he says."

But he could see in Mara's face that she'd already decided. "We've waited long enough for answers. I have a feeling I know what he's going to say. It's time for the truth...all of it. Let's go." She strode down the hallway.

"Strong lady," Jude said.

Levi didn't say it aloud, but his heart agreed. Strong, determined, amazing.

Mara took a seat opposite Teegan in the police interrogation room, trying to keep her breathing calm. Jude stood next to her, and Levi stayed outside, listening to the recorded conversation.

Teegan's skin was a ghastly gray, his eyes dull and sunken. "I had to see you. Thank you for coming."

"Don't thank me." Mara struggled to force the words out. "I am going to do whatever I can to make sure you're punished for what you did to my sister."

"Please," he said, almost a wail. "It was wrong of me to spend the weekend with her and not tell the cops. I led her on when I should have made a clean break of it, but I am telling you the truth when I say I did not know my father kept Corinne a prisoner. I believed the story he told me. I can't believe he made that all up. Something happened to him when my mom died. Part of him died, too. From then on, his sole focus was me, and it was smothering sometimes."

Mara recalled something Gene had said. *That kind of loneliness can blacken someone's soul.* She wasn't buying it. "If you didn't know about my sister's imprisonment, why did you run?"

He swallowed. "I didn't want to lose him."

"Him?"

"Peter. He's my son." Teegan gulped. "Mine and Corinne's."

Mara could barely get a breath in. Part of her knew it was true, but it floored her nonetheless. The little boy with the dark hair who sucked his fingers. Corinne's son. Her nephew.

"Can you explain?" Jude said calmly.

Teegan sucked in a huge breath. "Corinne contacted me, told me she was pregnant, but I didn't believe it. I refused to see her, just like I told the cops. Dad said six months after I told her off on the phone, she showed up and left the baby with him while I was out. Dad told me she'd been trying to raise him alone and she was tired of it so she brought him to us. It made sense to me except for one thing. I never understood how that shoe discovered in the national park fit in. Dad said she told him that weekend she came to spend with me..." His face colored. "Her bag was stolen by someone at the bus station. Whoever it was had taken her shoes, too." He swallowed convulsively. "Now that everything's come out, I think maybe my dad planted that evidence to make it look like she killed herself so the police would close the case."

"You never said anything about this before when you were questioned about Corinne," Jude said. "You and your father allowed the police and the Castillos to believe she was most likely dead."

"I... I'm sorry for that, but I didn't know what my dad did until just now." His face twisted, and he rubbed his palms over his cheeks. "I was telling the truth, that I never saw Corinne around the time of her disappearance. I told her on the phone to stop calling me. I thought it was a lie, but she was obviously pregnant when Dad imprisoned her. Put yourself in my shoes. I had assumed along with everyone else that she'd died in the desert and tried to get on with my life. Then one day months later, Dad walked into the kitchen with an infant in his arms and said—" his voice broke "—she'd come back and left the baby...my baby. I know I should have come forward then, so the Castillos would know she hadn't died, but Dad said we needed to keep it quiet." He looked at Mara. "Dad said if I told anyone that the baby was Corinne's, they would come back and start investigating again and we'd lose Peter." Tears spilled down his face. "I believed him. How could I not believe my own father?"

"Because your father told you to lie," Mara snapped. "He pressured you to steal my sister's baby."

He sucked in a breath. "He said your family would hate me if I told the truth, try to get involved in the baby's life, maybe even sue for custody or something, since Corinne hadn't turned up."

"You had no right to keep it from us." If her mother had known she had a grandchild? Of course she'd have wanted to be involved. And they'd never even had the chance. Mara and her parents hadn't had any idea that Corinne was pregnant; it never would have crossed any of their minds. "You passed my sister's baby off as Amelia's. She's in on this too."

He choked back a sob. "Once Amelia heard my dad's version of events, she didn't want to lie at first, but the doctors told her she has a problem with her uterus and she might not be able to have children. I told her to care for him for a week, and then we'd call the police if we had to and tell them what my dad told us about the last time he saw Corinne. Of course, a week was long enough for her to fall in love with Peter."

Mara shook her head. "Amelia is part of these lies. No wonder she looked uncomfortable whenever she was around me."

Teegan stuck his chin up. "Amelia has been a great mom to him from the beginning. It would kill her to lose him."

"Why did you run to the airport? Why now?" Jude said.

Shoulders sagging, he looked completely exhausted. "I got a text this evening. Dad said Corinne had come back, just appeared out of nowhere. I couldn't believe it… I mean I was just in shock."

Mara swallowed hard as he continued.

"Dad said he was sure she wanted to take our son. He told us to run and take Peter, gave us money. We were trying to figure out what to do—" he gulped "—when I saw Corinne running across the property, so thin and wild-looking." His face paled even more. "I figured I was seeing things. I started after her, but then Dad called and said there was a search warrant served. That was the moment I knew he'd been lying all this time. Lying…" His words trailed off and he shoved a hand through his hair.

"Corinne managed to escape," Jude said. "Stole a phone charger and ran. The Camp Town activity was keeping Gene busy. She saw her opportunity."

Teegan bowed his head. "Honestly, I did not know what my father did to Corinne. It was wrong, and twisted, but he only did it because he loves me."

"You know what?" Mara said, eyes glittering. "My father loves my sister, too, and your dad took her away and stole her baby. He's going to prison where he belongs."

"I know." His voice broke. "I'm so sorry. I should have told the truth. And I shouldn't have kept Peter from you." Teegan looked up at her. "But what about him? We've raised him since he was an infant. Amelia is the only mother he's ever known."

"It's not up to you to decide what to do," Mara said through gritted teeth. "That is going to be up to Corinne. Your father took her choices away, and now it's time for her to get them back."

NINETEEN

The night was split between the hospital and the police station. Corinne was heavily sedated, and though her condition was stable, there was little else they could report. Levi and Mara returned to the ranch as the sun was rising. The fire department had cleared the scene, but one engine remained in case of hot spots. The air stank of smoke, and the ground around the main house was scorched black.

"We kept it from spreading into the back of the house," one of the fire crew said. "Looks like just the front room, part of the kitchen and the porch are totaled. Some of your plants survived, too."

He thanked them and tried to swallow his grief. The front porch and surrounding grass was burned beyond salvage. "Banjo," he shouted again, praying he would hear an answering bark. Nothing.

The wood slats of the porch were blistered and

probably not safe to walk on. Had the animals crawled into the grass? As much as he wanted to believe it, he didn't think so. Banjo had been injured by Gene's shot, possibly a fatal wound.

Mara came up beside him. "I've called and called. I'm sorry. Maybe they ran for safety."

But he knew they hadn't. He nodded, turning away slightly so Mara might not see him blinking back tears. Banjo would have stayed, he would never have deserted his home. Just to be on the safe side, he pried up the burned slats of the porch, fearful of what he would find there. The injured dog might have burrowed under because he felt safe from the flames. Banjo was tough, he told himself. Had to be to survive being lost and starved and coming to land on a sad-sack ranch. But toughness only got you so far. He'd depended on Levi, on the ranch, to keep him safe. And so had Tiny and Rabbit.

Mara took his hand and squeezed. She probably knew he was on the verge of tears, and she was protecting his dignity by not expecting him to talk. The small hole made by Rabbit was now obstructed, riddled with burn marks, blocked where the charred wood had collapsed. The dog and kitten had probably crawled under the porch to escape the flames and died of smoke inhalation. Rabbit might be there, too. Had they been scared? In pain? Wondering why he did not come to save them from the flames? "I'm sorry," he murmured.

Mara caressed his shoulders. How could she have the energy for compassion after what she'd been through? They stood there, lost in their perusal of the wreckage.

The wood shifted, causing more of the porch to sink. More beams giving way? But the movement continued. "What in the world...?" He sank down and yanked some of the ruined boards away that were blocking the hole.

In a flurry of movement, something began to tunnel out from under the mess. Bits of soot and flecks of wood whirled, and they both shielded their eyes from debris. Banjo squirmed out, tail whirling like a propeller. He leaped at Levi with such wild joy that Levi fell over on his back.

"'Jo," he gasped. "You made it." Banjo swabbed his chin with an eager tongue. Levi hugged him close, laughing and rubbing his friend. When he could finally fend off the dog's unfettered slobbering, he got to his knees to examine him. Mara sank down to join him.

"Let me take a look at your wound, sweetie," she said, wiping at her own tears with the back of her hand.

There was a bloody gash on Banjo's shoulder, not deep but long.

"He'll be okay," Mara said. She accepted licks

from the limping Banjo who spread his hysterical attention between the two of them.

Levi hugged his dog. "I'm so glad you survived, buddy."

Banjo jerked out of his grasp and dove back under the porch again. To Levi's astonishment, he emerged with a soot-stained Tiny. He put her down at Mara's feet.

Mara scooped up the wee cat. "I can't believe it. Her ears are singed, but she seems okay." The little cat balled up in Mara's arms and began to mew plaintively. "Your Papa Banjo took care of you, didn't he?"

Banjo barked and disappeared again into the hole. This time Levi and Mara out and out gaped as the dog hauled a reluctant Rabbit from the darkness. Banjo barked twice at Mara until she put the kitten down next to him. The three of them, rabbit, dog and cat, sat together, six eyes staring at the humans. Banjo barked once more before he began to alternate between licking Rabbit's ears and the top of Tiny's head. Banjo, it seemed, had adopted another child. Rabbit endured one more lick before he hopped away, tunneling back under the porch.

Levi exploded with laughter. Mara joined in. They laughed until tears streaked their cheeks.

When their mirth had subsided, Mara wiped her eyes again. "I'll get some supplies and clean up Banjo's wound. I'll be able to tell if he needs stitches."

Levi watched her go, her step light and joyous. He realized he was experiencing a deep sense of peace. Why? His ranch was in shambles, and the buyer would surely offer less now that there was a fire-damaged house to be dealt with. Probably razing it would be the most feasible plan. Now both Mara's siblings were in the hospital, and a little boy's life was about to be turned upside down thanks to Gene's lies. Why should he feel that sense of peace?

But deep down he knew. It was because of the soot-streaked woman who was striding to him.

"Can you get him to leave off his grooming job for a minute?" she asked Levi.

"Wait." He took her hand, and she must have felt the tension it in, because she looked at him quizzically, settling the bag with the supplies on the ground. It was too hard to look at her and speak what was on his heart at the same time. He kept his eyes on the horizon.

"Mara?"

"Yes?"

"I'm about to lose everything."

"Oh, Levi. I wish you would—"

He stopped her with a squeeze. "Listen. I'm not a good talker so this is gonna be rough."

She went still. "Okay."

"I don't have the right to ask this. I'm gonna lose the ranch. It's all I ever wanted…until now."

"Levi," she started again but she trailed off when he turned to face her. His pulse almost stopped at the soft glow in her chocolate eyes. Would that expression turn to one of rejection? Could he stand it? Only one way to find out.

He pulled in a breath and forged ahead. "I never met anyone like you. You're the strongest woman I've ever known. Matter of fact, you're stronger than most men I know."

She cocked her head, birdlike, puzzled.

His stomach muscles contorted like a wild horse resisting the bridle. "What I mean to say is…" His mouth went south on him, and the words dried up. Was that perspiration on his forehead? He cleared his throat and started again. "I'm trying to say… I mean, I want to tell you…"

She reached out and touched his cheek. "Levi, deep breath."

He complied, but the wild horses stampeding through his insides did not slow down.

"Say it. I'm listening."

He inhaled the deepest breath he could manage. "I love you."

Her fingers stopped for a moment, then dropped away from his cheek.

"I don't have a right to have you. I'm going

to be broke." He sighed. "Even when I had the ranch I was always a broken tractor or a vet bill away from poverty. I'm not a good catch. I get my words all tangled up, and I don't know the first thing about building websites and writing newsletters." He held her hands, desperate to pull her close but fearing she would break away. "But I love you. I can't imagine my life without you in it. You're the best thing about my day, every day. You're the best thing that ever happened to me."

Now she pressed her lips together. To hold in her feelings? To stall until she figured out how to gracefully refuse? Cold prickles cascaded along his spine. He should say something. Anything. "I… I don't have a ring yet, but I can't wait." He fished in his pocket and dropped to a knee, pulling out the little sand-bottle necklace he'd bought. He unscrewed the top and dumped out the contents, filling it instead with some unscorched soil. "Now you'll always have some of the Rocking Horse. Would you marry me, Mara?"

Her hand fell away, and he panicked. She was going to reject him? Why wouldn't she? With everything going on in her life?

She considered him, head tipped to one side. "Marry you? My brother's best friend? A guy who eats ice cream for dinner and takes care of every stray animal that comes along? You, Levi Duke?"

"Yes, ma'am. That's what I am asking."

Now he saw her tears glistening. "I've had a crush on you since high school. God brought me here so I could understand the man you've become."

A spark of hope stirred in his chest. "I'm trying every day to be a good one, and I will do my best never to hurt you." But still he hadn't heard her answer. "I… I mean…was that a yes or a no?"

She laughed, a jubilant, joyous chortle. "I love you, Levi. Let's get married, why don't we?"

He swooped her into a hug that sent Banjo into excited barks. He hardly heard. He had no idea how the future would pan out, or what he'd embark on next, but as long as Mara was his wife, he'd be thankful every day of his life.

A million questions rattled inside him. Where would they go? How would he support her? Where would they live?

He put them all aside and relished that God had given him Mara, and He'd work everything else out in good time.

The next week passed in a blur. There was so much to be done between Seth and Corinne that Mara and her parents were constantly driving back and forth. She didn't tell them of her engagement. She thought that should wait until circumstances were more stable. Her sheer happiness was at odds with the knowledge of the trauma Corinne had endured. Her mother in particular was still trying to process what had happened to her youngest daughter. They would all need help to sort through it and, with God's help, move beyond it.

The mornings were spent with Corinne, and the afternoons she helped Levi as much as possible to clean up the main house so he could continue to live there, at least until the ranch was sold. She'd gotten a small hot plate hooked up in her cabin where she warmed meals for them and a teeny microwave to zap instant coffee. The poor quality of food didn't dent Levi's enthusiasm. Each meager meal she attempted was met with happy approval. She suspected she could serve him Banjo's kibble and he would still say how tasty he found it. Just thinking of Levi made everything so much easier to bear. There would be monumental challenges ahead, but her engagement bubbled like a clear brook inside her. The joy of it warred with the heartbreak, the sweet with the bitter.

The next morning she drove to the hospital in her brother's repaired SUV. The psychologist had been there the day before when they'd broken the news about Peter. Corinne had sobbed. "I showed up that day to talk to Teegan, anyway, even though he'd hung up on me because he didn't want to discuss my pregnancy. Teegan wasn't home, but Gene let me in. Before I realized it, I was locked up. Gene said I had no right to come and blackmail Teegan into taking care of a baby. He accused me of trying to entrap Teegan, that it wasn't really his baby. I tried everything I could think of to convince him. I begged him to let me go. I promised that I would never come back or contact Teegan again."

Mara gripped her sister's hand tight as the horrifying details spilled out.

"Gene fed me, visited me every day. I begged and pleaded, but it did no good. I even tried to hit him with a chair. He punished me by taking away the chair and not visiting me for two days." Her face crumpled. "I thought maybe he'd let me out when the baby was born. I don't know how he convinced himself it was justified to lock me up and take Peter away. After I delivered Peter, he told me…" She'd begun to cry again. "He told me Peter died, and after a while I believed it. He refused to answer any of my questions so I stopped asking. All these years I told myself he was dead, and I mourned my baby." Her tears turned into out-and-out sobs.

Mara joined her in her tears. "Oh, honey. I am so, so sorry."

"He watched me so closely. That's why I couldn't write a note on the postcard. There was no time. And the text… I figured he wouldn't know what *Marbles* meant, and that's all I could type before he almost caught me."

Mara had answered dozens of her sister's queries about Peter and shown him pictures, but the question remained about what to do going forward. For that one, Mara had no answer.

Her parents and ongoing support from doctors would help Corrine learn how to live as a free person again, making her own choices, extricating herself from the shadow of fear. At least Gene had not hurt her physically. "I think he liked the company," Corinne had said. He would come tell me all about what was happening, with Camp Town Days and stuff. He would cry, sometimes, that his wife was not there to share it." She sighed. "It was like I was his shoulder to cry on, never really my own person."

Today Mara greeted her sister with a kiss, happy to see she looked less pale and more rested. The plate in front of her indicated she'd eaten a little.

"Guess what?" Corinne said. "Doc says I can get out of here soon. He's recommended a doctor in Henderson to give me ongoing therapy."

"That's fantastic, sis." Mara held back tears. Life would begin anew now that both of her siblings would be out of the hospital. It wouldn't be the same, but they'd find a new normal somehow. "Is that where you want to go?"

She sighed. "For now. I want to be close to Mom and Dad. I think I've given them enough headaches for a while."

"You always were a problem child," Mara said, and they both laughed.

"You're coming back to Henderson, too, right?" Corinne said. Her look went sly. "Or is there someone you'd like to stay closer to? Levi, maybe? I saw him holding you in the hallway when the door opened."

Mara blushed. "We can talk about that later."

"Why not now? I've got no place to go."

"Because my love life shouldn't be your focus at this moment."

Corinne grinned, reminiscent of her saucy-teen days. "He popped the question, didn't he?"

"How do you know that?"

"'Cuz you're flustered, and you keep fingering that necklace and your mind wanders. You are a woman in love."

Mara was so pleased to see her sister's spark coming back that she did not mind the probing question. She was about to confess when there was a soft knock on the door and Amelia stepped in, holding Peter on her hip.

Mara froze. "I'm not sure this is good for my sister right now."

"No, please, come in," Corinne said, a catch in her voice. She struggled to a sitting position. "I want to see him."

Amelia's eyes were swollen and bloodshot, her face lined with fatigue that revealed sleepless nights. "This is—" she swallowed "—Peter." She cleared her throat. "He's a good boy, the delight of my life. He knows his alphabet, and we're starting to read together. His favorite thing is playing with trains with his daddy." She let Peter down on a chair, and he drove his little toy car along the seat, oblivious to the conversation.

Mara stood protectively near Corinne. "Why did you come here, Amelia?"

"I'm sorry. I know I shouldn't have. I've been on my knees praying about what to do. I did not know my father-in-law took him from you. I hope you believe me. I would never do that to another mother."

"I do believe that," Corinne said. "But you knew he wasn't yours, and you lied."

"I truly believed you'd left the baby because you didn't want him." Amelia bowed her head. "No excuse. I did lie. I'm sorry. I love—" she shuddered and gulped "—I love this little boy with all my heart and soul, but he is your child and I can't... I mean..." She began to sob quietly. "I'm so sorry. I didn't know. You were right there underground the whole time. I don't want to give him up—it's ripping out my heart— but it's what's best for him." She set him down, kneeling next to the child.

Amelia's whole body trembled, and she clung to the hospital bed with one hand as she spoke to Peter. Her voice came out strangled and tight. "Honey, this is Corinne. She's your—"

"Friend," Corinne put in quickly. "Hello, Peter. Nice to meet you."

Amelia stared, seemingly struck dumb.

"You are so handsome," Corinne said. "I understand you like to paint. I do, too. Could we paint together sometime?"

Peter nodded, peeking under his bangs at her.

Amelia stood, her hands on her mouth. Her voice was a whisper. "You...you aren't going to take him away?"

Corinne's eyes were wet, too. "I'm not sure what I'm going to do, but I know I can't be a parent to him right now." Her lip trembled. "You're a good mother to him, Amelia. I'm sure Teegan is a good dad, too, in his way. He wasn't good to me, he lied like Gene told him to, but I believe he didn't know that I was imprisoned, either." She gazed at Peter. "For now, you're what he needs. When I'm better, we'll work out how to do this, one step at a time. I promise, though, I won't cut you out of his life."

"Considering what was done to you…" Amelia choked back a sob, reached out a hand and clutched Corinne's. "I don't know if I could have been as kind as you are."

Corinne offered a shaky smile. "We'll try to explain it to him someday when he's a bit older. For now, I just want to know how he is, maybe see him occasionally while I try to put my life back together."

"Of course." Amelia nodded, still breathing hard. They had another minute of awkward conversation before Amelia gave Corinne a slip of paper with her cell number on it. "Come over when you can."

Corinne nodded as they left. She stared after them. "Did I do the right thing?"

Mara wiped her sister's tears. "I think you were amazing."

"And you'll help me figure out what to do?" Corinne whispered.

"Absolutely, one step at a time, just like you said."

"He's a handsome boy, isn't he? Smart, too, right?"

Mara looked at her sister, no longer a teenager,

but a woman, a mother, and a breathtaking one at that. "Yes, he is. I'm proud of you, sis."

Corinne smiled. "Thanks, Marbles. I learned from a good big sister. I'm glad I have you in my life."

"Me, too, Corinne," she said.

And then they both cried together about what had been lost and what they'd just rediscovered.

Mara was sitting at the card table which stood in place of the burned kitchen table, trying to help Levi decipher the forms the bank had provided to help with the sale of the ranch. She'd just finished feeding Rabbit. A few of the hydroponic plants had survived the fire, so he was kept in fresh kale. All the kibble had been incinerated, but the local vet had donated a few bags of kitten and dog chow when he'd heard of the fire. Laney and Beckett brought over several meals and a larger portable refrigerator. Levi, Austin and Jude had spent an hour constructing a temporary porch which the animals had promptly burrowed under. Several townspeople checked in and dropped off baked goods. The goodness of the locals warmed her heart. She only wished it would save the ranch.

"Does everything have to be in triplicate?" Levi grumped as he slapped down the papers.

"Seems like it," she said. She embraced him

around the shoulders and kissed his neck. "We'll get through it."

He sighed and raised his face for another kiss. "As long as I have you, I believe that."

They heard a car pull up, and Banjo set up a clamor.

"Another meal drop?" Levi said.

She laughed. "Let's go and call off the dog."

Levi whistled to Banjo who was circling the sedan. The dog obediently returned to his side.

"That's Dad," Mara said in surprise. Mara's father got out and helped his mother. They both opened the rear door and Corinne emerged. She was still waif-thin, but her eyes were not vacant anymore. Mara wrapped her in a gentle embrace. "Hey, sis. It's great to see you."

"Great to be seen." A mischievous smile lit her face. "Did you decide to burn the ranch down rather than sell it?"

Mara hoped the joke did not hurt Levi. He was already in anguish about the impending sale, especially since no one seemed to want the older horses. "I didn't think you were coming today," she said. They'd decided Mara would go home and get her family settled while Levi completed the sale. That was as far as they'd gotten on planning their own future. The wedding date could wait.

"We have a surprise for you," her father said.

He opened the rear passenger door and helped Seth stand. Leaning on a cane, he walked slowly to face her.

Mara squealed and ran to him. "You're out. Are you okay? How are you feeling? Does anything hurt? What did the doctors say?"

He laughed and dismissed her questions. "They agreed to let me out, that's all that matters."

Levi's eyes were wet as he hugged Seth and slapped him on the back. "You are a sight for sore eyes, buddy."

Seth grinned. "Aren't I, though?" He took in the burned house and the newly constructed porch. "Had to come see what you were doing to our ranch."

Levi's face crumpled.

"We can talk about that later," Mara said. "Let's go sit inside and have a soda."

Seth didn't move. His eyes narrowed. "Dad said you were making plans without me."

Levi exhaled. "I'm going to sell it, Seth. You need your money back."

"I don't remember putting you in charge of making my decisions."

"Seth…" Levi started.

"What I need," he continued, "is to use my muscles and regrow my strength. I'm going to do that here, riding horses and making trouble.

I talked to the physical therapists, and there are people I can see here in town that take payment plans."

Levi gaped. "No way."

"Yes way, Levi."

Mr. Castillo sighed. "He's determined, and that's what got him out of bed. If he wants to ranch and it makes him better, so be it."

Levi looked as though he was in shock.

"Guess that means you're not selling," Mara whispered through her tears.

"Selling?" Seth said. "No way. I'm gonna live in that shack right there, see, and leave the main house for the newlyweds once they get hitched."

Mrs. Castillo clapped a hand over her mouth. "You're getting married?" She rushed to Mara and hugged her and Levi tight.

"How did you know we were getting married?" Mara said, laughing.

"I've got this big-mouthed baby sister," Seth said. He winked at Corinne. "Don't worry, kiddo. I'm going to be traveling home plenty to make sure you aren't hassling Mom and Dad too much."

Corinne grinned. "Good."

Mara's mind spun with possibilities. Could she actually stay? Would they be able to make the ranch home? "Can you keep the store going without my help?" she said to her parents.

Mr. Castillo grinned. "We'll do our best. Besides, I am sure you'll be coming up often to visit your sister."

"Yes," Mara said, realizing she was crying again. "You know I will."

"All right, then. Looks like we've got a wedding to plan, a ranch to run and plenty of horses to tend to."

"Along with a couple of oddball siblings," Mara said, pointing to Banjo, Tiny and Rabbit who sat in the shade watching.

"What's a couple of more oddball siblings to add to the bunch?" Seth said.

Levi looked down at his boots, and Mara leaned in to him. "You okay?"

When he looked at her, she was lost in the breathtaking blue of his eyes. "Better than okay," he said. "I feel like I've finally come home." As he bent to kiss her, her heart agreed.

Home.

Finally.

* * * * *

Dear Reader,

Can you imagine a place as special as the Rocking Horse Ranch? Maybe there is no desert ranch in your life, but we all have those blessed places where we feel we belong. For me, it's a tiny garden here in suburban California where I sit and create my novels. My visitors are black bees, dragonflies, a couple of lizards and the hummingbirds who visit my blossoms. The space is tiny, noisy and blessed. No matter where we are, a sprawling wilderness or a wee little backyard, God can find us there. I hope you have enjoyed the second installment of the Death Valley Justice series. Most of all, I pray that you are safe and healthy and able to find that special place where you can feel God's presence in your life.

Thank you for reading my book. If you'd like to know more about me or my novels, you can visit me at danamentink.com. There's a physical address there if you'd like to write, or you can find me on Goodreads and Facebook. God bless you, friends!

Dana Mentink